To Kevin

"to the ma̶... is no end, ... to them is wearisome to the flesh"

Ecclesiastes 12:12

♡Crista x

parenthesis

[

First published in Great Britain in 2006 by Comma Press
Comma Press, 2nd Floor, 24 Lever Street, Manchester M1 1DW
www.commapress.co.uk

A CIP catalogue record of this book is available from the British Library

ISBN-10   0 9548280 7 0
ISBN-13   978 0 9548280 7 3

The publishers gratefully acknowledge assistance from the Arts Council England North West, and the support of Literature Northwest, which is itself assisted by ACE NW and CIDS (The Creative Industries Development Service), Manchester.

Set in Bembo by XL Publishing Services, Tiverton
Printed and bound in England by SRP Ltd, Exeter.

Contents

No Closure

All short stories have a flaw. Deep in their programming, coiled in their moment of conception, there's a glitch. A bad command-string. A contradiction. From this flaw grow many others — useful, generative ones; the conflicts that any plot, in any type of narrative, has to resolve. But with short fiction, underpinning such surface tensions, there's a more fundamental conflict; a special kind of spanner in the works.

In drawing together any new anthology of shorts an editor quickly learns to spot this glitch. The stories that stand out, that buoy up in the fading memory of the slush-pile, aren't simply those that possess the best writing, line by line, or most memorable characters or ingenious plots. The ones that stay with you are the stories that niggle, that aren't quite right (in the realism sense of 'right'), and aren't quite right in a short-story-shaped way.

The first thing the glitch must do, of course, is keep the story short. Brevity cannot be a mere whim or accident of composition, it must be inherent in the first idea, like a radioactive half-life, making any extension of the material or lengthening of plot impossible without destroying the story. Moreover it is the *way* the glitch renders stories unsustainable or unstable, rather than the mere fact that they are, that defines them.

We might think that one way stories do this is through 'orality' — as the critic Mary Louise Pratt called it. That is, the frequent allusion in short fiction to the act of narration, to the process of being spoken. As Pratt notes this can be anything from 'the incorporation of oral-colloquial speech forms in the language of narration... to instances where the whole text takes the form of represented speech.' By feigning speech, a short story automatically commits to shortness; as it must be believably spoken in one sitting.

Indeed, of the twenty stories collected here, twelve are first person narratives – each with touches of colloquialism and allusions to the act of delivery – while one is entirely in the second person. Several are fairly drenched in the speech patterns of their narrators: John Carnahan's 'Bread and Autism' blurs the strange syntax of its characters' dialogue with that of the narration. Paul Brownsey's 'Out There' is made up entirely of speech, mixing one side of a conversation with read-out-loud emails. While L.E. Yates' 'Lucky and Unlucky' is a single, imaginary address from one lover to another, reliving an event.

Pratt's 'orality' won't do as a defining glitch, however. It is a long way from being the most important thing these stories do, structurally. It tells us nothing of the shape of the stories *being spoken* and is far from exclusive to short fiction. Many novels deploy 'orality' very effectively. All they require is a small leap of faith with regard to what is realistically 'utterable' – the sort of leap of faith that any art (or artifice) requires.

Infact artifice gives us our first clue as to what the short story 'glitch' really is. Literary conceits, over-arching metaphoric devices and unlikely, even incongruous, ingredients are peculiarly common to short fiction. In such stories sheer contrivance is almost enough on its own to captivate the reader and draw him or her up the gradient of a story – through the simple intrigue of when, where and how the contrivance will collapse (for it must), not to mention why it was chosen in the first place.

Some stories have such a high content of artifice, or unreality, they offer themselves as an immediate sub-species of the short – the 'artifice story' – the archetype of which would have to be Kafka's 'Metamorphosis'. There are examples of it here as well: Tracey Emerson's 'Flesh and Promise' and the opening salvo from Adam Marek are both highly, and artfully, contrived, whilst demonstrating that not just any contrivance will do. The conceit has to be random, unlikely, preposterous even and yet, somehow, perfect. Take the decision in Marek's story to smash together entirely incompatible genres: literary realism and sci-fi fantasy. The decision always seems illogical, like a malfunction in the fiction programme (a cockroach? why a cockroach?) but, in retrospect, it's an incongruity that couldn't have been better chosen.

This sense of part of the story being 'wrong but right', unexpected and arbitrary but serendipitously perfect, is something that any regular short story reader will be familiar with. It allows us to be quite exact about what the glitch is in the 'artifice story': it's the illogicality of something otherwise perfect for reflecting, symbolising, informing and ultimately *telling* the story in question.

The demands of most literary realism, however, rarely allow anything so straightforward.

In realist short fiction, the most common way that brevity is hard-wired into a story is through the withholding of a part of the narrative – a hidden, suspended narrative, whose absence is ultimately unsustainable (it's only a matter of time before it drops into view). This 'buckling' version of the short story is by far the most dominant species, and constitutes the vast bulk of the realist short fiction canon. It was first hinted at by Chekhov when he confided his instinct to focus on the ending of a story and 'artfully' concentrate there an impression of the entire work. The Russian formalist B.M. Éjxenbaum put this idea more vividly, when he claimed the short story 'amasses all its weight *towards the ending*. Like a bomb dropped from an aeroplane, it must speed downwards so as to strike with its war-head full-force on the target.' What's actually speeding down towards the ending is the missing part of the narrative, often a single fact, a lie, a hidden life or concealed part of a character, that rewrites everything. Typically the best stories of this type are those where, despite being inevitable, the arrival of this missing part is utterly unexpected.

The traditional 'twist story' is the most obvious example of this form, whether spelt out at the end by a Sherlockian character within the fiction, or by a turn of events, or the narrative's own calculated release of information. Gregory Normington's 'The Ghost Who Bled' (*Prospect*, Apr 04) and Jeremy Dyson's 'We Who Walk Through Walls' (*Never Trust a Rabbit*) are two well-turned examples of this recently revived tradition, and many stories play with the tactic here: Crista Ermiya's 'Marginalia' turns our understanding of the central character on its head; Paul Brownsey bluffs and then double-bluffs his characters' (and our) expectations throughout. In Anna Ball's contribution, it's a twist of familiarity that drops onto us.

The best of these stories don't so much tie up loose ends as snap them shut, like the claws of a mantrap around the reader. The ferocity of their snatch is primed by the weight of the heavy, suspended 'missing narrative'. Mere surprise isn't enough, of course. The twist, when it comes, has to re-illuminate all that's preceded it – giving life to what was previously just latent by locking with it, perfectly.

Despite the much talked-of sea-change from traditional (action-driven) shorts towards modern (internalised) ones, the epiphanies of Joyce and the re-evaluations of Carver are not, structurally at least, that far removed from the traditional 'twist story'. In Carver we typically have an unforeseen reality about a character dropping into place – like the unexpected sensitivity of the speaker in 'Cathedral' who for the most part has seemed thoroughly intolerant. In the epiphanies of *Dubliners*, the endings are even stranger. Take 'Araby': a boy pines feverishly for a girl on his street and longs to buy her a token of his love; yet, right at the close, standing at the stalls with money in his hand, he simply can't bring himself to do it. These are only 'twist stories' minus the mystery genre's signposting and the final explanation; 'twist stories' where we have to do the retrospective fitting-together unaided, usually in the moments *after* the story has ended.

There is a type of realist story, however, that claims not to work in this buckling way at all, suggesting there may indeed be a glitch in the Glitch Theory.

The critic Eileen Baldeshwiler has identified a distinct sub-species of realist short fiction in her essay 'The Lyric Short Story'. Although she ascribes to this type many non-exclusive qualities – 'internal changes, moods, and feelings', 'the condensed, evocative, often figured language of the poem' – she also lists a more fundamental difference. In distinguishing the 'lyrical' from what she calls the 'epical' story, she claims that the latter type culminates in 'a decisive ending that sometimes affords universal insight', whilst the lyrical 'relies for the most part on the open ending.' From the twentieth century, she appoints such champions to this lyric school as Katherine Mansfield, D.H. Lawrence, Virginia Woolf, Sherwood Anderson, and early John Updike.

At a recent short story festival at Charleston, the writer David Constantine volunteered his own name to this list. 'There's no word in the dictionary I hate so much as "closure",' he confessed, by which he meant stories that 'tie everything up at the end with a neat bow.' As a writer, Constantine strives for stories that are not only open, but continue to open after you've finished reading them. This blossoming, as far as Constantine's writing is concerned, spreads from a central, inspiring image – one that haunts as much as is attended to, throughout the story. Examples of such generative images are easy to identify in Mansfield's work – the aloe tree at the close of 'The Prelude', the eponymous 'Fly', the corpse in 'The Garden Party'. Likewise in Constantine's recent work: images of dammed or backed-up water and ice seep through almost every story in *Under the Dam*. And there are as many lyrical, story-centring images in this anthology: the sight of a man walking on glass in Mandy Sutter's story; the insanity of the drinks trolley in a Scottish wood in Paul Hocker's 'Bad December'; the vision in L.E. Yates' story of the speaker's lover, spotted over a crowd of heads in tube station. Compared to such abiding, irreducible and seemingly stumbled-upon images, the idea of a central, predetermining 'glitch' smacks of a decidedly 'closed' view of the short.

It's a very real distinction Constantine and Baldeshwiler are making here, if only in structural terms. The lyric story creates a single atmosphere – like that created by the strange autism-speak in John Carnahan's story. This atmosphere is established early, sustained throughout and merely rings louder in its absence after the close. By contrast the epical (traditional and revelatory) story places all its chips on the ending. A useful way of comparing the two structures is to follow D.S. Mirsky's thinking when he described Chekhov – that progenitor of both realist schools – as plotting a curve of emotional processes in his stories which for much of the story 'seems to coincide with the straight line' of what's expected. Initially this curve only deviates through infinitesimal hints and clues, but ultimately shoots off exponentially. Mirsky's analysis may be true of the Joyce/Carver story and indeed traditional 'twist stories'; but for the majority of the lyrics, it's quite the opposite. The lyric story by and large makes its bid for transcendence early on and, if anything, launches straight for that height, bending into it with an image that resonates long afterwards:

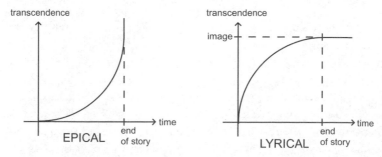

Such geometries are nonsense, of course, but they might illustrate why the champions of 'open' short stories are so passionately against closure. The expected 'straight line' of a mere sequence of events and its perpendicular 'meaning' – what C.S Lewis called the 'story' and the 'theme', what Roman Jakobson called the 'syntagmatic' and the 'paradigmatic' – could themselves be plotted as X and Y axes on a damned graph. Any deviation from 100% realism – the flat axis of the expected – is of course essential for story-ness, and in the case of most (i.e. epical) stories the ending is where we find the steepest deviation. As Frank Kermode puts it: 'Endings are always faked'. Realising this, the lyric writers strive to establish their fakery (i.e. their art) much earlier than the ending, so as to leave the reader with the pure, lingering effect of it, unfettered by the awareness of 'steepness'.

The problem with this reading is that, as well as sounding rather dismissive of 'epical' stories, it arguably misunderstands quite what these stories do. A good end-heavy story, while balancing realism and design, is never actually aspiring towards the abstract or the non-temporal (through its temporal means). Even the most unexpected *Dubliners* epiphany *isn't* strictly evoking anything as ambitious as eternal truth, or as Baldeshwiler puts it 'universal insight'. When we try to work out why the speaker in 'Araby' can't bring himself to buy a token for his love, we have to play the extra-textual Sherlock and extend the remit of the story beyond the text (as we do with Carver), beyond even what we can infer of the character. We have to widen the orbit of evidence into our own experience – memories of our own infatuations and their complexities – so as to have a sufficiently complicated set of evidence to make both the story and its ending somehow consistent. The wider narrative we have to draw down, to accompany and explain the revelation, is our own narrative. By this we aren't extending the story's remit to infinity or to 'universal insight', we are merely adding ourselves to it.

Short stories don't aspire to permanent truth, merely longer truths; ones that go beyond the events that occur in them, and stretch out into the lives of their characters in both directions. There's even a type of story that's specifically designed to appear infinitely long – what we might call the 'chain story' – whose revelation is that the apparent one-off incident it narrates is in fact one of a chain of countless repetitions. Tobias Wolf's 'The Rich Brother' is a classic of the type, and there are elements of it here in the stories by Pat Winslow, Alice Kuipers and Melanie Mauthner. But even here, the *ad infinitum* allusion to permanent truth isn't, actually, anything so ambitious; it merely asks us, at the end, to try and contemplate a *wider than expected* narrative.

Ultimately the 'openness' of a story is measured by how much the reader has to contribute to it (and this is never as dichotomised as Barthes would have it). In the 'twist story' our contribution, though aided, is a real one: we, the reader, must work out how the withheld part of the narrative locks together consistently with the previously given part. In the revelations of Carver and Joyce, the process is much the same, we merely have less clues to piece together. With the lyric story, and the task of resolving the central image, we have perhaps to contribute most. But in all cases openness is a matter of degree.

More importantly, so is closed-ness. In first conceiving a lyric story, the author's faith in the central image – whose meaning even the writer cannot fully resolve – is itself a pre-ordination. The versatility of that image, its refusal to collapse into straightforward, finite meaning (as well as its ability to abide alongside the ordinary) is what no doubt convinces the lyric author that there's a story here in the first place. In this much its eventual shape is pre-determined; its strangeness is in the blueprints, coiled in the conception.

In both schools of realist short fiction the glitch is a hole where there shouldn't be one. In the epical story it's a gap in the plot or characterisation, a parenthesis through which a revelation drops. In the lyrical short it's a textual puncture, a tunnel burnt through the far side of the story by an otherwise everyday image.

Only the first of the three forms we've looked at, the 'artifice story' of Kafka and co., truly straddles the lyrical and epical sets. Like the lyrical, its atmosphere (of oddness) is established early on and the effects linger long after the close. Like the epical, there's a final twist we have to come to terms with, namely the dawning, unexpected appropriateness of the artifice itself.

We shouldn't be that surprised, of course. Somehow it's right that this key conflict in contemporary short fiction only be resolved in fantasy or surrealism. It's appropriate that a Grand Unified Theory of the glitch, of 'the right type of wrong', can only be attained once realism has been thoroughly abandoned. It's some glitch.

Testicular Cancer vs the Behemoth

Adam Marek

The ground shook, and a sound like thunder shot through the city. Austin felt the vibrations travel through the floor beneath his feet, and up the legs of the chair on which he sat. He'd never been so afraid. My world is ending, he thought.

The doctor looked around, as if the source of the tremor could be found within his office. 'You should have come as soon as you noticed the lump,' he said. 'I'm not a specialist, but your cough and backache indicate that the cancer may have spread from your testes to your lungs and lymph nodes.'

Austin looked at him, and the beginnings of a word formed on his lips, but the rest of his body was inert, and no sound escaped him.

'I'm sorry Mr Weaver,' the doctor continued. 'I'll make an emergency appointment for you at the clinic. In these circumstances, they'll fit you in tomorrow. I'll call you later at home to confirm a time.'

Austin stood up from the chair, and the ground wobbled beneath him. He ached. He could feel the cancer dissolving him. He thanked the doctor and left. The people in the waiting room stared at him as he walked through, and he wondered whether they'd heard what had been said. Why couldn't it have been one of these people? he thought.

Outside, the sun was baking the street, melting ice-lollies, making people crazy. Austin watched the pavement as he walked. He was half-aware of people running past him, of screams and exclamations. Two cars collided, and then a third drove into them, but Austin barely noticed. The ground shook again, and he stumbled.

The pain in his balls was unbearable. He had another hour until he could take pills again, but he couldn't wait. He saw a hotdog vendor racing his cart along the street, looking back over his shoulder. Austin chased after him.

1

'Can I have a bottle of water please?' he asked, struggling to free his wallet from his pocket while keeping up with the vendor.

'Are you crazy?' the vendor said. 'Get out of my way.'

'I just want a bottle of water, come on, stop a second, I'm dying here.'

'Get out of here,' the vendor said, then huffed to himself and opened up the freezer compartment, still running, and pulled out a Coke.

'I can't take painkillers with Coke,' Austin complained.

'I don't care,' the vendor coughed. 'Take the whole lot.'

The vendor pushed the cart off the side of the pavement and then broke into a run. Austin followed the cart to where it rolled into a parked car. He fished around in the ice and found a bottle of water. The ice compartment smoked in the hot air. He wanted to crawl into the compartment and switch himself off. He fished a blister pack of pills from his back pocket and unscrewed the lid of the bottle. A woman in high heels ran into him, glancing off his side, spinning round and hitting the floor. She yelped as she fell, and one of her heels pinged off.

'I'm sorry,' Austin said. 'I didn't –'

The woman picked herself up before Austin could stoop down to her. She kicked off her shoes and ran barefoot. He watched her weaving through the hundreds of other people running in the same direction, but the sight meant nothing to him. Nothing made sense anymore. He looked at the woman's shoes on the pavement. A man in a dark suit, tie loose around his neck, jumped over them as he ran to the car that Austin stood beside. He stabbed his key into the lock and looked at Austin.

'Is that your cart?' he said, climbing into the car, sweat and panic all over his face. Austin shook his head. 'Get it out of the way, now, move it.' The man gesticulated with his arms. Austin just stood there, watching reflections of people moving across the windscreen in front of the man's face. The man honked his horn, and Austin stepped back onto the pavement. The man slapped the steering wheel with both hands. He turned the ignition on and pushed the cart out of the way with the car. He made a five point turn, crashing into a parked car and a lamp-post alternately until he was free and sped off in the same direction that everyone was running.

Austin popped two pills. He thought about Margot, his sister. She lived about ten blocks from there. As soon as he thought about her, he needed to be with her. Margot would make sense of it all. Margot would bring comfort.

Austin floated down the street, while the stream of people flowed around him, often bumping into him in their desperation to get past. The booming sound continued every couple of minutes, like the slow heartbeat of the city, shaking the ground, making Austin flinch. The sun was right above his head, its rays frying his blonde hair, cooking his pale skin, making freckles. His face leaked sweat, and his shirt was wet against his neck. He guzzled the remainder of the water. Looking up at the sky, he wished it would rain. He wanted the sky to crack open and wash away the heat and sweat and rinse the cancer from his body, flush him out and make him new again.

This can't be happening to me, he thought. It's some grotesque mistake. Austin had first felt the lump six months ago. He had been in the bath, holding his balls for comfort, when he'd felt something irregular, like a dried pea. He rolled his balls between his thumb and fingers and felt it again, a hard lump on the side of his right ball. He'd felt sick all day thinking about it. He knew if he went to the doctor, he'd have it chopped off. And he wondered what would happen to his sex drive if he only had one ball, or no balls? What if they had to remove both? So he left it. He would go next week when things weren't so hectic at work, when he'd been with Molly for a little longer. They'd been together for less than a year. It was too soon to be going to her with things growing on his balls. She would be disgusted. There never seemed to be a right time. There was Christmas, and then the cluster of family birthdays that occurs in February. In March, the pain started, first a dull ache, then getting worse every week. The pain terrified him. He suspected that he had testicular cancer, but he didn't want to go to a doctor and have it confirmed. While he didn't know for certain, he might not have it, and everyday that he might not have it was a luxury.

A month ago the pain became unbearable. He was taking paracetamol and ibuprofen pills together every four hours from the moment he awoke. He couldn't concentrate at work, and it was difficult to pretend that everything was alright when he was out with Molly. After six months, he decided that he couldn't wait any longer and made the appointment. But now it was too late.

Margot Weaver, Austin's sister, lived on the seventh floor of an apartment block. The corridors were full of people charging about with suitcases and the sound of television sets blaring from open doors. Someone had stuck chewing gum to the floor outside Margot's door, and he kicked at it while he waited for her to answer, releasing a stale minty smell.

'Austin,' she said, her eyes wide. 'What are you… thank God you're alright. Have you just come from outside? Did you see it? It's all over the news. I've been worried sick. Mum and Dad are here too.'

Margot was still in her pyjamas. He felt a spring of tears begin to form in his eyes and blinked and blew at them to hold them back. How was he going to tell them all?

The apartment smelled of coffee, and there were half-full cups and packets of biscuits all over the table. Mum and Dad were sitting on the sofa, perched over their knees, the faint flicker of television light shining on their eyeballs. They flashed him a quick glance as he stepped into the room, then returned their attention to the television.

'Can you believe it?' Dad said. Austin hadn't seen Dad for a couple of months, and he looked older than he remembered him. A wisp of white hair evaporated off the top of his head. His checked trousers were too short and riding high up on his calf, revealing thin ankles, but the way he hovered on the edge of the couch, and the way his hands massaged each other made him seem full of energy. 'They say it's heading this way. I just hope it gets full before it arrives.'

'We should go,' Mum said. Mum was wearing a powder blue jogging suit, which she always wore around the house, but Austin had never seen her wear it outside her home. She smiled at him briefly and looked back at the television.

Margot touched Austin's elbow and smiled sympathetically. 'Would you like some coffee?' She asked.

'Sure, and a big glass of water. It's baking out there.'

'You've been outside?' Mum asked.

'Yes, I just came in,' Austin said, perplexed.

'How far did you come? Did you see it?'

'I've just come back from the doctor. It's been a rough morning. I got –'

'Doctor Stewart's?' Dad said. 'That's quite close; did you see anything?'

Margot shuffled back into the room in her pink Muppet slippers. She fixed her eyes on the television as she handed Austin his coffee and spilled some down the back of his hand. Austin wiped his hand on his trousers. He cradled the hot cup in his palms and stared into the milky surface of the coffee, watching the reflection of the ceiling light ripple and break apart.

'Why are the lights on and the curtains closed?' he asked. 'It's the middle of the day out there.' They all ignored him, transfixed by the television. Austin looked at the screen. There was a monster movie on. A giant lizard was tearing up the city. Why are they watching this? he wondered.

'Is Molly on her way?' Mum asked.

'Molly? No. She's at work.'

'I doubt she'll be working. She's probably on her way home. You should give her a call.'

Austin's brain turned in his head. He couldn't make sense of things anymore. Maybe the cancer already had its feelers in his brain. He looked at the television again. Why are they watching this stupid programme? The film was done in a real-time docu–drama style. Jerky camera movements, shot on video to make it look like the news. Icons in the corner of the screen. Panicked anchorwoman. Everything. The cameraman was set up on top of a building about half a mile away from the monster. The monster was barely visible within the cloud of dust and smoke. Buildings had been smashed to rubble around it, twisted spires of metal poking through the devastation. A flat-roofed factory was punctured where the monster had stepped straight through it, and from the hole sprang orange fire and black smoke.

The streets around the monster had been emptied, and military vehicles had moved in. The soldiers looked tiny against the backdrop of the giant lizard, which stood upright on its hind legs, slapping buildings into powder with its enormous tail. The soldiers were setting up a tall barrier in a perimeter around the monster. They had missile launchers and heavy machine-guns pointed at its scaly belly.

'Why would Molly be on her way home?' Austin asked.

'Are you drunk, Austin?' Dad said. 'She works over that side of town. People have been fleeing in this direction all morning.'

'Fleeing?'

'The monster.'

Reality flickered for a moment, as if his sister's apartment was on television, and a spike of electricity had rippled the cathode rays. He looked again at the television screen, and at his family glued to it. It couldn't be real. And then he remembered the people running on the street, and the loud booming he'd heard from Doctor Stewart's office. He felt pain in his head as he understood, as if the mental leap he'd had to make had snapped a few synapses. His ears fogged up, and he could hear his heart coughing blood around his body. He retreated inside himself. Saw his organs pulsing and jiving, fluids rushing around, and his genitals, blackened and swollen, wheezing.

'The monster, Austin,' Dad repeated.

The monster. Austin looked at the television screen again with new eyes and saw familiar landmarks. The sign of the Halcyon Hotel, which was visible from Molly's office. The golden dome of the mosque. Peppard's toy store. And amongst them, the monster, muscled and green, a crest of short spikes running from the top of its head to the end of its tail. Its skin, like an iguana's, hung in saggy folds around its armpits and thighs, a suit of armour, and the military's bullets appeared to have little effect.

'This is real?' Austin said.

'Get this boy some more coffee, Margot,' Dad said. 'Yes, it's real. How could you have missed it?'

'I had other things on my mind. So how did it happen?'

'It came up out of the sea, just crawled out and started smashing up the city. They think we're safe over this side though. The military say they can take it down when they've cleared the area.'

Austin's muscles twitched with excitement. His balls, which had been like infected melons, dragging him down, shrank to peas. In the light of the monster, they were almost insignificant. And for that moment, he was released from their burden. Thanks to the monster, he stopped dying for a second.

'So what distracted you so much that you couldn't see a giant lizard?' Mum asked.

'Is everything okay,' Margot asked. 'You look green.'

'Everything is fine. Can I borrow your phone?'

Austin dialled Molly's mobile number. It rang six times before she picked it up.

'Where are you?' Austin asked.

'I'm downtown,' she yelled. 'In Osma's.'

'You're downtown?'

Mum and Margot shifted close to Austin and clung onto his elbows.

'Can she see the monster?' Mum asked.

'Can you see the monster?'

'I can't hear you,' Molly said. 'The monster is just behind the Sony building.'

'Tell her we're at Margot's,' Mum said.

'Are the military there?' Austin asked.

'I'm trapped,' she said. 'I couldn't get through the exits. There were too many people. Some of us tried to find another way out, but the monster blocked us off. We're hiding out. My battery's almost dead. I've got to go.'

And then she rang off.

'What happened?' Margot asked.

'She's downtown, in the kosher bakery on Beazely Street.'

Mum put her hand to her mouth and her eyes went watery as she looked at Austin. Dad looked at him for a moment, then turned back to the television. They all looked at the screen. A camera mounted in a helicopter moved around a column of smoke to reveal the monster. It was thrusting its arm into a tall building and pulling out handfuls of people, desks and light fittings to eat.

'I'm going there,' Austin said.

'You can't,' Mum said.

'Don't be so stupid,' Margot said. 'You'll be killed.'

'You'll never get past the barrier anyway,' Dad said.

Austin looked at them, and listened, but his whole body felt tugged by the magnetic force of the monster. He had to get close to it. If anything could cure his testicular cancer, then standing in the presence of the monster would do it, like standing in the shadow of a mountain, his own shadow would be obliterated. He guzzled the remainder of his coffee, kissed his family goodbye and ignored their protestations as he left.

The city was twitching with panic. Now it all made sense. The people were fleeing, migrating uptown. He climbed into Dad's black Saab, swooning in the heat. The leather scorched his back, and he leapt out, opening all the doors to let the small breeze that flowed through the city carry away some of the heat. He watched the heat distortions pouring out of the open door, and listened to the sound of gunfire in the distance, and a great booming sound, like a landslide, like the monster had pulled a whole building down to its foundations.

The inside of the Saab had barely cooled when he got in, and he wound all four windows down. The steering wheel burned his palms. The cold fans blew hot for a few minutes until air rushing through the front of the car cooled the machine. The only good thing about the heat was the driving seat – the warmth flowing from it soothed his aching balls and allowed him to concentrate on the road.

The journey downtown was like swimming upstream. Cars and people flowed uptown, away from the monster. A couple of times, when the roads were wide enough to allow two cars to pass, he had a clear run, but most of the time the streets were narrow with cars parked on both sides and people driving away from the creature. They hooted and gesticulated at him as he tried to bully his way through them. No one wanted to give way. At first he was careful of Dad's car and leaned out of the side window to check he had room to squeeze between the cars, but he was conscious of how much time it was taking him to get downtown, and he began ploughing through, popping the headlights and drawing scrapes down the side of the black paint. When he could see the military barrier ahead, and tried to get out of the car, the door was so buckled that it wouldn't open, and he had to climb through the window.

Downtown was devastated. The air was full of smoke and brick dust. He ripped the arm off his shirt and tied it around his face. Powdery grains of fallen buildings collected on his eyelashes. The gunfire was loud and punctuated by explosions as the military fired missiles at the monster. Above this though, was the sound of the monster. Its roar hadn't come through on television. It sounded like a rusted iron ship being dragged across an enormous blackboard. It bypassed his ears and went straight to the centre of his brain, where it reverberated and made him feel nauseated.

The barrier was ten metres high, shining grey in the sun. People ran, tearful and dirty, through three doorways within it. Soldiers in helmets and goggles with big guns shooed them through, one at a time. When they emerged they were weak from struggling against one another, and stumbled as they ran for safety.

Austin wiped the sweat from his forehead. His feet were swollen in his shoes. His shadow was small around his feet, like he'd started melting and leaking out the bottom of his trousers. He skirted around the edge of the barrier, looking for another way in. He found more exits, but they were the same as the first three – packed with people trying to escape. The barrier broke at one point to allow the shops of Hayman Street to pass through it. This section of barrier had no exits and no guards. The barrier stopped half way through Brannigan's sports store. The lights were out and the doors were locked. Austin picked up a wine bottle, which sat in a doorway, and hurled it into the display window. The point of impact veined out and fell back, like a net catching the bottle. Then the top section of the window dropped down in one sheet and smashed the bottom section into fragments. It was so loud that the silence afterwards was startling. Austin leapt through the broken portal before anyone came to investigate. He kicked footballs and trainers out of the way, jumped down to the shop floor, and walked through to the other side of the shop, on the inside of the barriers. He grabbed a baseball bat from a tub and hurled it at the window. A huge keyhole-shaped section collapsed, and he nicked his shoulder as he slipped through it. Blood fanned out across the shoulder of his shirt, fuelled by the sweat-soaked material. Salt in the wound stung.

Hayman Street was deserted. Dust and ash and smoke filled the corridor of shops. Austin knew the way to Osma's: he and Molly used to meet there for lunch when they first started dating. Austin walked because the heat was too oppressive to run. He took the smaller streets, where the shops and offices were closer together and gave more shade.

He was only two streets away from Osma's when he ran into a patrol of soldiers. They were dead, crushed by a lump of concrete the size of a van. Austin grimaced when he saw their blood sprayed outwards, mingled with the dust. The soldiers' guns were pinned beneath the rock with them, but one had been thrown out across the ground. A soldier's arm stretched out towards it, as if he were reaching for it, or had been throwing it to safety the moment the rock fell. Austin picked up the big gun. He swung the shoulder strap over his head and held the gun like he'd seen in the movies. He felt great with it, a little cooler, in control, sharper.

Osma's was deserted. The shop door was wide open. The smell of bagels and rye bread was intoxicating against the smells of smoke and gas outside.

'Molly?' Austin walked towards the back of the shop.

'Austin? What the –'

There were sounds of bare feet climbing a short flight of stairs, and then Molly appeared through a doorway. Her dark hair was messy and stuck to her face. She held her high-heeled shoes in her hand.

'What are you doing here?' she said as she hugged him. Austin linked his arms behind her back, but only for a second. It was too hot to hold each other. They kissed, and Molly's face tasted salty. She touched the blood on his shoulder with concern.

'I came to rescue you. Look, I have a gun and everything.'

'Where did you get that?'

'I found it. We should get out of here. There's a route through Brannigan's. We don't need to queue for the exit.'

'Austin, I can't believe…what did you –'

The monster bellowed, and Austin's brain quivered in his skull. The beast's scaled foot slapped down outside, and threw the bakery into shadow. Austin was mesmerised. The three front toes were truck-sized, with talons that raked up the tarmac.

'We've got to get downstairs,' Molly said.

'It'll crush the whole building.'

'We can't go out there. There's nowhere to run.'

The building shook as the monster tore a chunk out of the roof. Plaster dropped down around them. The monster shifted its weight about and the ground trembled, making them dizzy. The sound of helicopters came.

'The soldiers will be here in a minute,' Molly said. 'We've just got to wait it out, downstairs.'

'We won't be safe there. The monster could bring the whole building down into the cellar, and the military are going to bomb the crap out of this area. They think they've cleared the zone, so they can do what they like. You make a run for it, and I'll distract the monster for a moment.'

'Don't be ridiculous.'

'What's going on?' a man said, climbing to the top of the stairs and stepping out onto the shop floor. Two other men and one woman were behind him, peering out fearfully. One of them shrieked when he saw the foot outside.

'We're going to make a run for it,' Austin said. 'The whole place is coming down.'

'We can't go out there,' one of the women said.

Everyone ducked down and threw their arms over their heads as the monster tore down another chunk of the building. Half the ceiling crashed down around them, filling the air with dust, setting off electrical sparks. The monster seemed to have sensed that there were people in the building, and was poking one of its long green fingers through the roof, probing. Austin turned to face the door, and using the shield of his back to stop people seeing, he massaged his balls. The painkillers were wearing off, and the ache was returning, flowing out of his groin, washing against his stomach and his legs.

'We have to go,' Molly said.

'Brannigan's is only five minutes from here,' Austin turned to face the group again. 'You can climb through the broken window and then out the other side of the barrier.'

'You lead the way,' Molly said.

'I've got the gun. I'll hang back and make sure it doesn't follow.'

'A gun is useless against that thing. Put it down, Austin, you look ridiculous.'

Austin felt a pang of embarrassment explode in his stomach. He'd been running on adrenaline since he left his sister's house. He had felt like a hero. He'd gone to rescue his girlfriend from the monster. His shirt was torn. He was covered in dust and blood. He had a gun. Could Molly not see that? He thought about kissing her on the mouth before they left, but her comment had soured him. He didn't feel like kissing. He wondered whether he should have come for her at all.

Molly and the others shuffled through the rubble to the door, careful not to step on any fallen wires. A helicopter, buzzing overhead, had captured the monster's attention. The group seized the moment and ran from the shop.

Austin ran with them a little way, but the pain in his groin was too much. It was making his legs weak. He couldn't run. He watched Molly from behind as she ran away, her curly hair bobbing on her shoulders, her calves tensing and flexing, her feet bare. He wanted her to turn around and see what he was about to do, but maybe it was better that she didn't. She'd only try to stop him.

The monster slapped the helicopter. It spun round, a mangled heap, and exploded before it hit the ground a few blocks away. Austin walked back towards the monster. He raised the gun up to eye level, but it was too heavy. He held it down at his side, with the strap round his shoulders supporting the weight, like he'd seen in the movies. His finger was wet against the trigger, and almost slipped as he squeezed.

The gun rattled and shook as it spat bullets, but he held tight. The noise shook his eardrums into numbness. The vibration shot all the way up his arms, into his head, making his vision blur. It rattled his stomach too, and soothed his aching balls. He had the gun aimed at the monster's groin, and he kept the trigger depressed. A constant stream of bullets fired out of him, into the monster. Ribbons of blood spattered out from between the monster's legs. The monster tried to advance on Austin, but he stepped back and kept on firing. As his body shook, it became one with the gun, one with the monster, one with his testicular cancer. Nothing mattered anymore. Years of anxiety, all the things he'd ever worried about, were shaken out of him. His sister and his parents fell away from him. His job. The city. His car. The time he'd spent working for things that would never reach fruition. His unhappy schooldays. Everything came apart and dropped away, leaving him pure and fresh. Empty and beautiful.

Static

Pat Winslow

I don't like it when they show someone new in. This one's a student. He uses long words. He wears glasses. I wear glasses. He has a book.

'Tell him what to do Mickey.'

I won't tell him. I don't like it when they bring someone new in.

'Hi,' he says. 'I'm Toby.'

He wants to shake hands with me. You have to shake hands sometimes. It's not polite if you don't. My hands are sweaty. His are dry.

'How long have you been here, Mickey?'

It isn't Mickey. It's Michael John Walker. I hate it when everyone calls me Mickey. I won't tell him. I'll just show him the brush. There are two. Mine's got MJW on it. I wrote it myself. The other brush has MUFC and WANDERERS ARE SHITE. Someone drew a woman's privates on it and there are men's privates as well. I don't know why men like drawing men's privates. They do it all the time.

'I like Wanderers,' the new man says. 'Who do you support?'

There are two chairs. My chair's got MJW on the back. The man sits on the other one.

'What's that hole for?'

There are two holes. One in the ceiling, one in the floor. The one in the ceiling is by the big long window. The one in the floor is by the door at the other end. The room is made out of wood. Wood's normally brown but it's old so it's gone grey. When it rains I have to put the light on. Mr Jenks says the light should always be on for health and safety reasons. But I like saving the planet so I only turn it on when it's dark. I always turn it off when Mr Jenks leaves. Toby turns it on.

'That's better,' he says. 'Mind if I read?'

It's a French book about some people in a room. He says it's about hell.

'Do you believe in hell, Mickey?'

13

I've got a newspaper. I read it from the middle. I put the kettle on. When it's finished boiling I'll be on page nine, then I'll put the coffee and hot water in and add five sugars and some milk. Toby hasn't got a mug. He didn't know he had to bring one. There are some plastic cups on the shelf from last time. I don't want to make coffee for him. It's not what I'm paid for.

After page nine it's page eight and they start getting ready upstairs. I've never been upstairs. They get more money upstairs. The noise gets closer and closer and then it gets loud and all of a sudden the metal thing slides back and the polystyrene bits come rushing down through the hole. It's nearly up to the ceiling when it stops. Toby's chair is near the pile. Two bits have landed in his coffee. Toby says shit and tries to get his cup before any more go in. He knocks the cup over and the coffee goes on the pages of his book. Toby says fuck fuck fuck like the last bloke did. Fuck fuck fuck and I know he's angry with me so I carry on sweeping and pretend not to notice. I sweep the polystyrene over to the hole near the door. It takes a long time. The polystyrene is static and sticks to the brush. It sticks to my hair and clothes. Sometimes it makes ticking noises and if it's dark you can see blue sparks. I like it when there are sparks. That's another reason I don't like to turn the light on.

Toby gets his brush and starts sweeping next to me.

'Sorry,' he says. 'I didn't mean to frighten you.'

He touches me on the back of my arm between my elbow and my shoulder. People are always doing that. Mr Jenks does it. 'There's a good lad,' he says. I'm thirty-four. He wouldn't like it if I did it to him.

When we've finished, Toby puts the kettle on and washes our cups.

'More coffee?'

He puts the milk in first and then the sugar and then he adds the coffee and stirs it fast till all the granules have gone.

'It makes it bubbly. Look.'

He pours the water on.

'It's frothy,' he says.

'I don't like frothy coffee.'

He shrugs and sits down and starts doing the crossword in his paper. I pour mine down the sink and start again.

'What do you like?' he says.

On page seven there's a picture of a squirrel that died when it fell on a cactus. All the spines went in its stomach.

'Do you like chocolate cake?'

I've got cheese and tomato sandwiches, a packet of crisps and a can of Coke on the shelf. I'm a vegetarian. We only get half an hour for lunch. The people upstairs get the same. Mr Jenks goes to the pub. He smells of beer and onions when he comes back. Sometimes he's drunk. He came in once and fell asleep whilst he was talking to me. I had to sweep all around him.

'Shall I get us some chocolate cake?'

Next to the squirrel is an article about an asylum seeker who has three mobile phones. I don't like mobile phones. They give you cancer. Toby keeps talking to me so I don't get to page six before the polystyrene comes down again. I don't know why he has to talk all the time. The last bloke didn't. No one ever talks all the time. Not even Mr Jenks when he's drunk. I can't get my work done properly. I can't read the paper.

'Is this what you do all day? Don't you get bored?'

Questions and more questions. I haven't reached the front page and it's lunchtime. I'm glad when he goes out. But Mr Jenks has to spoil it by putting his head round the door and checking I'm alright.

When Toby comes back he's got a cake and some apples. He has to use a biro to cut the cake in half. I don't want to eat any because the biro was behind his ear. Toby leaves my half on the tinfoil tray. He says I might want it later. He makes me another coffee and I pour it away. Then Mr Jenks comes in and shouts at Toby for being late.

'It's half an hour,' he says.

Toby says that's against the law. He says he's going to report the factory.

'You do that,' says Mr Jenks.

'It's not fair on Mickey here.'

'Mickey's fucking lucky to have a fucking job,' says Mr Jenks and he burps and walks out.

'Never mind,' says Toby. 'Have some cake.'

'I don't want some cake.'

'Christ,' says Toby and he throws my half down the hole by the door.

'That's a waste.'

'You should've eaten it then.'

It's fucking this and fucking that all afternoon every time the polystyrene comes. At half past three the door opens and a man I've never seen before walks in.

'Thanks mate,' he says and he walks out again.

Toby says it's probably the bloke from downstairs. He must have eaten my half of the cake.

'I didn't know there was a man downstairs.'

'Who did you think dealt with all the polystyrene then?'

'I don't know,' I say.

'There must be loads of us in this building sweeping it from one end of a room to another. How many floors are there?'

'I don't know.'

'What do they do with it?'

'I don't know.'

'Haven't you ever wondered?'

'No.'

'Christ.'

He sits down again and starts reading his book but the pages are all stuck together. He flings the book across the room. Suddenly I get an idea. I pick his book up and throw it down the hole.

'Thanks mate,' the bloke downstairs yells.

Toby goes ballistic.

'What did you do that for?'

The bloke downstairs is standing on a chair looking up at me. He gives me the thumbs up sign and I give him one back.

'It's French,' says Toby. 'He can't even read it.'

Toby's got the brush in his hand and he's getting angry. I'm scared he's going to hit me with it.

'What did you do it for?'

He's waving the brush around and the end of it smashes the light bulb. The glass goes everywhere.

'Oh for fuck's sakes. Now see what you've made me do. Help me clear it up before Jenks comes in.'

It's not my job to sweep broken glass so I go and sit down and read my paper. Toby comes over to me and grabs me by the shoulder.

'Clean it up you little shit.'

His face has gone white. His fingers are pinching my skin.

'Listen if Jenks comes and sees what's happened –'

The bloke downstairs is laughing.

'It's French,' he shouts up through the hole.

'Come on, Mickey. Clean it.'

'No.'

'What sort of crap is this? I can't read a bleeding word.'

'CLEAN IT!'

'It's not my job.'

'CLEAN IT UP!'

He shakes me so I start punching him.

'I'm not a little shit. I'm thirty-four. Your cake had bits of ear in it.'

Whack.

I'm a big bloke.

I'm much bigger than him.

Whack.

Sometimes it surprises me how big I am.

Whack whack whack.

I push him down the hole.

He starts crying.

'I've broken my arm.'

The man downstairs keeps telling him his book's in French but he's not listening.

'I've broken my arm, Mickey.'

'Do you read this stuff?' he asks him.

'Call Jenks, Mickey.'

'No way,' I shout through the hole. 'No way José.'

The bloke downstairs climbs onto his chair and looks up at me.

'José's crying,' he says. 'What shall I do?'

'Have you got a hole down there?'

'Yes,' he says.

'Push him down it.'

He gives me the thumbs up sign and I give him one back.

There's a scuffle which goes on for a little while and then there's a crash and a thump and everything goes silent.

'Is he gone?'

The man who ate my half of cake climbs onto his chair again.

'Yes,' he says.

He blinks and wobbles a bit then gets his balance.

'What's your name?' he asks.

'Michael John Walker.'

'I'm Kevin Bradley.'

He puts his hand up and I bend down and shake it.

'I'm pleased to meet you, Kevin.'

'Pleased to meet you. How long have you been here?'
'Fifteen years.'
'Blimey.'
'How long have you been here?'
'Twenty.'
'Blimey.'
He looks at me and blinks.
'He didn't last long, did he?'

Flesh and Promise

Tracey Emerson

We made a grand entrance. Show stopping.

Heads rotated in the busy bar, voices dropped as Marion gripped the chrome banister and began slinking down the stairs.

The perfect match. My beautiful new woman, her long hair dark and coiled and trailing over bare shoulders. A displaced romantic heroine. Myself, foreign and exotic – a dream fragment you clutch on waking.

'Drink, Madam?' A Korean waiter, probably hired for his cheekbones, offered Marion champagne and crossed her name from the opening night guest list.

Chattering bodies pressed against us as we moved into the bar. Bodies in black. Clean, modern cuts of linen, cashmere and satin. They stared at the woman in the red silk evening dress, weaving a rogue thread through their dark crowd.

The lighting in the bar seemed designed for flattery, giving everyone a temporary glamour. The usual opening night brigade. Freeloading journalists, actors, councillors, family and friends.

And then Fiona appeared.

Hair dark beneath the cropped blonde, a black knitted dress wrapped tight around the shape she has become. She stood by the bar, eyes jumping from her watch to the piano player at the white grand. A wave of her hand and the evening's modern jazz soundtrack began.

She hadn't expected to see me again. Obvious from the way she jumped at my reflection in the mirror behind the bar. The unmistakable red of me, the red of hearts, of lips, of blood.

She turned quickly, as if we might disappear. We didn't. She scanned the bar left to right, then ran to look over the balcony at the restaurant. Looking for Joe. Without success but her pale face told me he'd be here soon.

'Marion... you are a goddess.'

'Rees... stunning job, as always.'

Insincere kisses – one, two.

Rees's presence explained Fiona's. His bar and restaurant, her interior design. She liked working for Rees, finding relief in his world of minimalism and hollow chit-chat. Choosing materials, co-coordinating colours, arranging furniture – all keeping her away from home and Joe and what should have been.

Rees slipped his arm round Marion's waist, wanting to touch me. People usually do. His dry palm fluttered from bodice to skirt.

'Where did you get this, it's divine?'

'Well...'

Two young men waved from the stairs, distracting Rees.

'Sorry darling... beauty calls.'

Marion headed for the bar. Fiona stopped halfway through the list of instructions she was giving the barman and watched us closing in.

'Excuse me.' A woman blocked our path. 'I just have to say...' More compliments, another stranger's caress.

Fiona looked up as a group of new arrivals clattered down the stairs. Still no Joe. Safe for now.

'Isn't the décor divine?' gushed Marion. Her new best friend nodded. They cooed over mirrors framed with Perspex cherubs, grey tiled tables, chocolate leather seats and everywhere the glint of chrome.

So unlike Fiona and Joe's first home. A low cottage full of pine and patchwork and the happy patterned textiles Fiona used to make. Now she rips at wood and cloth, replacing them with slate and steel.

The woman went in search of her next best friend and Marion reached the bar, waving her empty glass. Fiona stood six feet to our right, a gap soon filled by a panicking Rees. He pointed out a waitress offering canapés in her harsh Australian accent.

'Agency,' explained Fiona.

'I can't have a woman with roots serving my guests.'

Fiona smiled as Rees stalked the girl through the crowd and sent her back to the kitchen with words that made her blush.

Hard to believe we ever fitted together, Fiona and I. With Joe alongside her in his vintage dinner suit, the image was complete. Beautiful couple, beautiful future and soon they wanted to start a beautiful family.

'Just think,' she'd said, stroking me gently, 'I might not get into this next year.'

But she did, looking elegant as they dined with Molly and Tim, celebrating their oldest friends' good news. When Molly proudly refused wine with dinner, Fiona's stomach tensed and shrank away from my soft reassurance.

A year later I could no longer stretch around her, but there was no dinner in honour of the failed operations and flood of hormones that had made her swell and ripple beneath me.

'I'm an architect.'

Marion had a new admirer. He'd snared her with a plate of sushi and the offer of a barstool. His right hand lingered against me as he helped Marion onto her seat.

Fiona watched as I showed Marion off. That's my skill. Knowing which body parts to hide and which to reveal. Knowing how to fold and hang around them. I slipped aside as Marion crossed her legs. They are good legs and I let the architect see them.

Fiona adjusted the sleeves of her knitted dress. Did she miss my sensitivity, my ability to bring comfort and confidence? Nothing mass-produced could ever do that.

'Excuse me,' said Marion. The architect had failed to build a good impression.

We were escaping to the toilets when we passed Joe, arguing with the Korean waiter. Molly and Tim stood awkwardly beside him. Fiona had spotted them too and exhaled deeply as Marion disappeared behind the glass and chrome toilet door.

How long would it take Joe to recognise me? I wanted to get back out there but Marion fussed over herself at the mirror, touching up a surface beneath which little lurked. Not a thought for me – she didn't even smooth out my creases. At least Fiona had always shared the limelight.

When we emerged, an ageing TV producer pounced on Marion, claiming to have met her somewhere before. Joe had his back to us, talking to Rees.

'She said she'd put them on the guest list.' Joe pulled at his waistband. He'd squeezed into his faithful dinner-suit, the trousers just a little too tight now.

'Not a problem.' Rees smiled at Joe, then glared at the offending waiter.

'Lovely venue,' offered Tim. 'We've not been to one of your places before.'

'Really?' said Rees, taking in Molly's floral skirt and Tim's insipid chinos before leaving them with a glass of champagne.

Joe muttered something to Molly and Tim, who laughed nervously. The three of them surveyed the party, grimacing at the dizzying improvisation coming from the white grand.

And then he saw me.

Smiling, he stepped forward but Marion's face confused him. He searched for the face that should have matched the dress and found it hovering by the half-open kitchen door. His head swivelled back and forward. Black to red. Red to black.

'I think baldness is quite attractive actually.' Marion was trying her best with the TV producer.

Molly and Tim steered Joe to a free table, putting space between him and Fiona, who'd retreated to the bar. A standoff.

That's how I ended up there tonight. A standoff. After three years of chasing the family dream, they'd agreed to stop trying.

'Just for a while,' said Fiona, 'we need a break.'

They played at fulfillment. Who needs kids? Fiona made interiors pretty for other people while Joe turned his drawing hobby into a full-time living, illustrating books for other people's children to read.

It's dangerous to leave gaps between you and someone you love. Trouble gets in.

The black infiltrated slowly – trousers, skirts and tops.

'I need them for work,' she told Joe. He didn't push her. They'd been together so long, arguments were pointless games of noughts and crosses that neither would win.

'They all look the same to me,' he said as Fiona struggled to choose between three black polo necks. She said nothing, knowing there were many shades of black and she'd felt them all – every single one of them.

The TV producer abandoned us. Marion sipped her drink, flat with this brief lull in attention.

'Hi.' Joe had come in search of answers. 'Sorry, but I have to ask...'

Molly and Tim approached Fiona. She pretended to let them distract her as Marion told Joe where she'd found me.

'A charity shop, you're kidding.' Joe looked me over, my identity confirmed by the tiny stain on my hem, the style of stitching round my waist. Surely he could see it now. How Fiona had slowly tunnelled out of the marriage, dismantling the past and throwing it away in pieces too small for either of them to notice.

'I just need a bit more room,' she told herself, ripping old favourites off their hangers and shoving them in bin liners. The black bags would sit in the spare room wardrobe and when Joe was out, she'd take them to charity shops all over town.

On our last night together, Fiona had to sit through another dinner for Molly and Tim. They were apologetic for their good luck.

'Don't be silly,' Fiona said, 'I'm absolutely delighted for you.'

Neither of us enjoyed it. I am made for curves and the glide of one buttock against another, but we'd grown apart, millimetre by millimetre, my bodice visibly loose around her bony back.

The next day she buried me in a bag with the other outcasts – fuchsia pink jumper, purple velvet jacket, green tracksuit bottoms. All the colours of the rainbow, jumbled up for jumble. Then she took us to a shop and left us there.

'Oh, the colours are gorgeous, very sophisticated.' Marion leant towards Joe as she wittered on about the surroundings. I refused to move this time, keeping her well covered.

'My wife's the designer.' Joe pointed out Fiona, floundering with Molly and Tim, the three of them glancing sideways and up and down in search of conversation and lost intimacy. 'Come and meet her.'

Joe crossed the room, the truth he'd feared walking bright red next to him, clinging to a body as full of flesh and promise as his wife's used to be.

He introduced Molly and Tim first. They shook hands with Marion.

'And this is my wife, Fiona.' Fiona nodded, tugging at her sleeves again. 'Isn't Marion's dress wonderful Fiona?' asked Joe.

'I really should get on.' Fiona tried to excuse herself.

'You won't believe where she got it,' he continued. 'Tell her Marion.'

Vanity and alcohol shielded Marion from the tension.

'Well I was in town a few days ago…'

She began the not so remarkable tale of finding a fabulous dress in a charity shop for next to nothing. Rewriting my history, the real story of my conception vanishing. I would no longer be raw, red silk bought by Fiona and Joe in India and carried in a rucksack through South East Asia. Who would tell people that the Bangkok tailor who made me, using Joe and Fiona's design, had only three fingers on his left hand? Who would know that Fiona first wore me to walk on a moonlit Malaysian beach? The beach where Joe, barefoot in his dinner suit, finally asked her to marry him.

'Give us a twirl Marion,' urged Joe, 'show us the back.'

Marion obliged, sprinkling champagne as she spun.

'Oh look Fiona,' said Joe, 'how unusual.'

He pointed out three red silk lilies at the back of the bodice. They were his idea – Fiona's favourite flowers to cover up the hooks and clasps.'

'Lovely workmanship.' His fingers stretched out to touch the lilies and stayed there.

'I'm sorry.' Fiona pushed past, letting her hand trail and catch me. The three of us reconnected. Just for a second but I am handmade and exquisite and felt it all.

And then she was gone, escaping into people and music and small talk; the little black dress taking all her pain and stitching it into its fibres, putting it on display for everyone to see.

Violins and Pianos are Horses

C.D. Rose

There's a town that sits on an elbow of the Danube in the top right hand corner of Bulgaria, but to call the town 'Bulgarian' wouldn't really be true. Any day there you would once have heard ten or twelve languages spoken in the streets. There was the Turkish of the Turks, the demotic of the Greeks, the Ladino of the Sephardic Jews and the German of anyone who'd spent time in Vienna and considered themselves to be one rung up on the social ladder. The Bulgarian of the Bulgarians themselves mixed with the tongues of Circassians, Gypsies, Albanians, Armenians, Rumanians from across the river and Russians from the other side of the Black Sea.

What the Composer still calls Ruschuk, though since he has been away people have come to call it Ruse, or Rousse, or Russe, is a town made up of the way it speaks, of the way it sounds. What the Composer still calls Ruschuk was and is a rusty old river port where timber is shipped out and grain picked up, a stopover on the way to Sofia or Vienna or Varna. It is a place whose inhabitants will refuse to classify as Eastern Europe, because the east always starts just east of where you are, but neither is it Central Europe as the town cannot be said to be central to anywhere at all, nor does the word 'Balkan' suffice because right now, as the Composer comes back to the place where he was born 84 years ago and where he hasn't set foot for the last 35, the word is beginning to spell 'trouble' once again.

It is to this noisy, invisible town that the Composer returns nearing the end of what he suspects, but does not yet know, will be the end of his life. It wouldn't be true to say that the Composer has been in exile all these years, as he doesn't really know if the travels that his life has consisted of really were an exile or not, as he left of his own accord and simply never wished to go back until now.

The first thing that strikes him about Ruschuk after so much time in the West is the sight of a working horse. His daughter offers him her arm as they climb out of the taxi which has brought them from the station to the Hotel Plaza and together they are splashed by the muddy water from a puddle disturbed by the hooves and spindly legs of a small pony. The pony, a strange animal with significant elements of donkey, is pulling a rickety trap run by an old man who looks identical to the old men the Composer remembers from so many years before. Next to him sits a boy, his son, presumably, or grandson perhaps, in a tired pink nylon shirt, not ever so different from the youths he has seen on streets in Paris, London and New York. The old man casually lengthens his arm and strikes the animal across its flank with a long black stick and it breaks from a hobble into a lame trot.

With one arm linked around his daughter's and the other clutching his own stick, the Composer and his daughter limp into the foyer of the hotel where they are greeted by soft lights and anonymous music, as though they had crossed the threshold back into what was once called the west.

They take dinner together in the restaurant where he is disappointed to find that they have no *banitsa* or *kavarma*, but settles for an admittedly fine piece of pork, and they sit in silence throughout with his daughter occasionally tutting about cholesterol. Irene eventually starts asking him questions, wanting to know how he feels, what it's like to come back, but the Composer brushes off her enquiries, irritated by the American twang of her voice, by the upward swing of her affirmative sentences, questioning and vulnerable. He is also irritated, he knows, because he doesn't know what to say, he has no responses to her demands, he hardly recognises this place he has come back to as the place where he was born, and also because the sight of the suffering beast on the road is still disturbing him, like indigestion. For a distracted moment he was tempted to throw his arms round the horse and weep, filled with admiration and pity for its depleted strength. It strangely reminds him of his own experiments with preparing pianos, opening up the box with a coffin-like reverence, seeing the thing's sinews and bones laid out before him. Is this how the horse would end up too? Its hair used to make blankets, its flesh used to feed the poor, its bones boiled down for glue. This is what the boy or his father or someone else would do with their horse when it finally collapsed and refused to move any further, just as the gypsies who had come past their house every Friday when he was a child had done. To break the silence that had fallen he began to tell his daughter how fascinated and frightened he had been by the gypsies, how he'd heard that they stole children, so was careful to watch them, hiding around the corner of the house, while they sat cross-legged on the dirty floor of the yard. Their maid took food out for the gypsies while they would sit and smoke and some would play music on ragged violins with scarves tied around their necks, punctured lung accordions and a ruptured drum.

The Composer says goodnight to his daughter and goes up to bed leaving Irene alone in the bar. Before he falls into a fitful sleep he thinks of how she had been stolen from him, not by gypsies, but by a different life, by schools in Paris, clothes shopping in London, by America, her home now. His experiences are so far from hers. Though she is a grown woman now, their lives seem to have no bridge that joins them, only one that marks a separation.

When he finally falls asleep he dreams uneasily of the horse he had seen in the street. He dreamt he was a child again, out walking the streets of a town that was still Ruschuk, though they were now lined by huge windowless hotels. He was with his father. The land around seemed flatter, silent and lifeless, bathed by an eerie stage light. The same trap passed by them and splashed them again, and some people with vague, indiscernible faces gathered round them to laugh at them. The driver took out his stick and began to beat the horse as if punishing it for its misdemeanour, until the horse's swollen belly became a drum keeping some brutal rhythm. The faceless people began to sing in tune with the rhythm, a wordless, howling song which got faster and faster in time with the horrible drum until words started to form. They were willing the horse back up again, trying to make it go one last stretch as far as the knacker's yard. He asked his father to make the Friday gypsy violinist come and play, hoping that his music would be able to make the horse get up, get better and walk again, then dance, then fly, then take the violinist flying after him.

Next morning the Composer woke feeling feverish and wondered if he was starting to fall ill. How would Irene manage if he fell ill here? She doesn't speak any of the languages. The hospitals are probably terrible. He remembers his mother coping with five children after his father had dropped suddenly dead one day, aged 40, less than half his age now. He had become the father for his brothers until, aged 16, he left for Vienna to study music, encouraged so much to do so by his mother who then spent the rest of her life blaming him for having deserted her.

Going down for breakfast he finds Irene already seated at their table and laughing far too loudly with the waiter who had also been the barman the evening before. She introduces him to Sorin, who in turn introduces himself to the Composer in English. Sorin offers to take them around the town, but the Composer declines, in Bulgarian, telling the boy that he already knows the town, though they both know this to be a lie.

They set out again on foot from the hotel, not really knowing where they are going but with the vague goal of finding the Composer's childhood home. He wants to show it to his daughter; as if to introduce her to the grandmother she never knew.

They get lost on a busy road somewhere outside the Metro superstore before Irene finds their way back into the centre of the town again and they end up in a park where the Composer thinks he remembers playing with a hobby horse. The memory is like a smell, waking up things he'd thought had been forgotten before they'd even been remembered. A hobby horse he remembers, a present from an uncle in England who had later drowned at sea.

They walk along a long street which he thinks he recognises though all the buildings on it are unfamiliar to him. Eventually they find what he thinks is the house where he was born and knock on the door. The Composer still has the key to the old house in his pocket. His mother gave it to him when he left and told him that he would always be welcome to come back, whenever he wanted to. He has kept the key for all these years, but looking at the lock on the door of the house as they hear the footsteps inside of someone coming to open it, he realises that the key would not work. The locks have been changed.

A short overweight woman wearing a worn blue apron comes to the door and tells them that the house has been divided into flats, and that she can't possibly let them in. They hear the sound of some children fighting within. The woman says that the house was only built fifty years ago anyhow, so it couldn't possibly be the place they are looking for. She shuts the door on them without saying goodbye.

The Composer and his daughter walk off again arm in arm like a four-legged creature, partially propped on the Composer's black walking stick. He doesn't communicate his grief to his daughter. They have taken away my memory, he thinks. Obliterating those old buildings erased his own memory, as well as that of the town. He still somehow expected to be recognised by someone, to find some old family friend to welcome him back home, to ask after his mother, his brothers, his sisters. At least to be known of, if not welcomed back.

He wanted to go back to the house and tell the slatternly-looking mother that he, the Composer, was described in the Grove Dictionary of Music as having been a disciple of Schoenberg, as having studied at Darmstadt, then having broken with Stockhausen and become one of the first residents at Ircam. He wanted to tell them that he, the Composer, has seen seasons dedicated to his music in concert halls filled with earnest audiences from Tokyo to Stockholm to Seattle, audiences that he will even admit, continued to dwindle as his music became more complex. He, the Composer, he wanted to say, was one of the first to be a serialist, and then one of the first to be a post-serialist, to go atonal, to even use old folk melodies and find himself accused of cultural misappropriation. He wouldn't have told her that the Grove Dictionary of Music also said that the Composer had followed an 'intriguing intellectual stairway that unfortunately had proved to lead nowhere.'

Nowhere? Here? Back to a Ruschuk that he couldn't even recognise or name anymore.

'This place is a fucking dump,' says Irene.

Irene doesn't want to spend the evening in the hotel again, so they go out in the late afternoon and find a café in the town centre. Sorin the barman has recommended the place to Irene. Recorded music is playing loudly – the Composer recognises an old Rumanian song sung by a squealing child with an electronic thump thump thump behind it. He asks if they can sit outside but Irene says it is too cold. He is pleased to see that there are men as old as he is in the bar, a few sitting alone, others with younger men. He thinks that he must have known them as children, perhaps gone to school with them, but recognises none of them. Irene is the only woman there.

The boy in the grubby pink nylon shirt reappears with a group of men, some the same age as the Composer, others almost young enough to be their sons or grandsons. They are all carrying instruments – a violin, an accordion, a double bass, a cimbalom and a trumpet, and they start to play. They make several false starts, one instrument beginning then stopping, getting as far as picking out a melody or rhythm on its own before realising that the others are not keeping up. There is much discussion between them. Eventually they start together, but fall apart after a couple of bars as they come hopelessly out of time. They argue openly, shouting at each other. The oldest man looks uncomfortable, doesn't speak. The youngest wants to play as fast as possible. The bass limps and lopes forlornly, picking out sparse notes against the murmur of the bar. Again they start, separately this time, one instrument picking up after another, the sound gradually gaining force above the smoke and chatter of the bar. This time it doesn't fall apart. The Composer thinks he recognises the music, it was an old tune they used to make bears dance, and he dislikes it. The music stays together, and builds slowly. It reminds him of the cruelty of such shows and how they had upset him as a child. The music continues to grow, faster now. Yes, he remembers this piece, it starts slowly and gets faster and faster and faster. The musicians' hands and fingers move more quickly, in rhythm. No one in the bar is chattering now. The musicians' hands and fingers start to blur. The sound is too much, too loud. Some people in the bar whoop, yell, clap hands. The Composer dislikes it all immensely, its cheap sentimentality, the banal melody. And then the bass hicks up, seems to split into two, feet stamp. The music slips into a time signature even the Composer does not recognise. The trumpet shatters and plays overtones, as if it were two men playing the one instrument. The fiddler is deranged, surely. Or two instruments being played at the same time by one man. This is rough music, dirt music, music with one leg. This is a song their grandfathers taught them and that their grandfathers were taught by the Lord, the song their grandmothers wept to as they were bartered into marriage. The tinkling cimbalom finds its bass range and builds up like the thunder of divine judgement. The volume continues to rise. Everyone in the café is banging on tables, singing wordlessly. Stamping feet. Shouting. They are not accompanying, but all together creating the song, the sound, the music. The players, mad-eyed, blank-staring, lose themselves totally. They become deliverers, a mouthpiece for a sound that they are not creating, only reproducing. Automatons, sweat in their hair, blood in their eyes and madness on their fingers. They are playing to bring dead horses back to life, playing the spine of the skinny animal. They have become outside the music. They are no longer playing the music – it is playing them. They who have no voice find a voice in the voice of the music.

The music stops suddenly and almost no one applauds. The sound disappears like smoke. The musicians awake looking fallen, collect up their things and slope off. The Composer and his daughter throw them a US dollar, knowing how pathetic this is.

On his second night in the place he still wants to consider as 'home', though no place has ever felt less like home than this re-named Ruschuk, he once again falls into fitful sleep, his ears buzzing, and dreams of music, again. He thinks it may be the effect of mixing the gritty red wine he drank in the bar with the pills he has to take for his heart, but fears tinnitus, the musicians' nightmare, an affliction worse than blindness. All members of his profession dread Beethoven's alleged end, despite knowing that Beethoven wasn't really deaf, but beat his head against his piano after sawing off its legs because he was not able to get out the music he could hear in his head because the instruments to make it had not yet been created.

Tonight, the Composer doesn't dream images but sounds, a beautiful choir rising up out of the buzz in his ears, their voices singing Renaissance polyphony in spherical, celestial harmony. Their voices meet, merge, rise up to the heavens but as they ascend they start to fail, break and rasp around the edges. Strange harmonies interrupt, the time signature changes and the voices take on the sounds of the choirs of old women in the hills, moving eastwards, the wrong direction, southerly, until they become an Arabic wail. Nothing, he thinks lucidly during his dream, nothing he has ever heard is quite as beautiful and as unharnessable as this sound.

The music ceases and he now dreams nothing but the sound of the Ruschuk of his childhood, the babbling of tongues fading into the burbling water of the Danube until all is silence.

The next morning he goes down to breakfast again only to find himself seated alone at their table. He looks for the boy, Sorin, but he isn't there either. A polite waitress tells him that Miss Irene hasn't come down yet. The girl reminds him of someone, though he cannot think who.

After breakfast he sits in the lobby reading newspapers that he finds incomprehensible despite understanding all the words. He thinks of going to wake his daughter but knows better. She eventually appears looking ruffled around midday.

'I thought you'd have gone out by now,' she says, with a feigned look of surprise. 'Gone for a walk or something. You don't have to sit around waiting for me.' He remembers then who the waitress reminded him of.

A girl playing cello who he'd taught years before in Paris. She had come to a masterclass that he had given in his tall-windowed, white-walled apartment and stayed after the other students had gone. He had asked her to play for him. He remembers her face perfectly now, despite having forgotten it for so many years, but even though her dark-skinned, heavy-eyebrowed features are so clear he cannot even vaguely remember her name or where she was from. She could, of course, have been a gypsy. Her arm was tensed as it held the bow across the strings and she paused for a tiny moment, then took a sudden sharp intake of breath before she begins playing. He remembers seeing the hair under her armpit (a red dress, he remembers now, she was wearing a red sleeveless dress, it was hot, summer) and the thin line of sweat that formed on her upper lip as she bit down in concentration, her eyebrows just meeting in the middle as she wrinkled her forehead with the attack of the first note, the muscle taut beneath her brown skin, flexing as she held the neck of her instrument down, firm, tightly, and caressed it and scraped it with her bow, that unique mix of tenderness and violence, her face unbroken, a blank mask flashing into a split second of expression as the note went up, teeth behind her lips visible then to again, split, the sound of the amber body of the cello itself, sawing, buzzing, her eyes closed, her arm moving faster and faster up the neck, her movements becoming shorter, quicker, more precise as the sound became shorter, more intense, harder, sharper. After she'd finished she looked up around as if surprised to find herself where she was. That moment of letting the music play itself, of losing awareness of self and letting her hands automatically bring forth the sounds from a piece of hollow wood and taut strings.

The Composer remembered what it was that had made her playing so special, the grain in the sound, the sound of her body in the voice of the music, the points where the sound tensed and broke and twisted like a bend in the river, breaking free of its reins, oblivious of what was creating it. This was not ever music that had attempted to be pure, but was filled with the girl's body, the bones of her instrument, the sinews of its strings, music that was disturbed, mongrel, music that was not only itself, but also everything else. This was the music he should have written, he knew, though of course never did, this was music that could not be written perhaps, this music that he could only now capture through memory or dream.

Even though the Composer will be remembered after his death with retrospectives in Munich, London and New York, the gypsies look forward to a future playing in bars in Black Sea resorts and tube stations in Sofia, Athens, Naples, Rome, Paris, London. Their highlight will be getting called to do a prestigious show in an important club in Berlin which will finish with the accordion player getting violently drunk and swinging out at the violinist who has meantime tried to make off with the evening's bar takings before getting belted by a baseball bat that the barman keeps stashed for just such occasions.

But it doesn't matter because they know, like the Composer now knows, that violins and pianos are horses, made from the bodies of hardwood animals, their ringing tones empty ribcages with horse hair hobby horse manes dragged across horse head strings by gypsies from central Asia, strength and sweetness and mystery for those who can't ride a violin or play the horse, music to make horses dance, to make them move, to bring forth the sweetness from the strength of the animal, the tethered recalcitrance of taut scraping strings, the hollow ribcage of the four-legged piano, horse-shaped as the violin is horse-headed, a scarf tied round its neck. The sound kicks up dust as it crosses the plains and charges into Europe to hold Vienna by siege before being let in and tamed by expert riders at the Spanish school, stolen from its smelly thieving gypsy owners, cleaned and polished and painted and introduced into royal courts, then noble palaces, then bourgeois households, where it will be ridden by sullen children playing sulky quintets. But pianos and violins will never really be tamed, because there's always something about violins and pianos and horses that frightens people, something that disturbs them, because violins and pianos are horses.

The Art of Gutting a Fish

Anna Ball

The proper preparation of fish is a fine art that every good housewife must learn. The secret is simple: to be ruthless in gutting; for the thorough removal of all bones and undesirable innards will ensure a delicious dish guaranteed to please your loved one...
– from *The Newlywed's Introduction to Family Cooking*

It did not take her long to realise that, much like the cycle of tides, things functioned in certain ways along the coast. An imminent storm was announced by the sound of agitated water. A fisherman's marriage was foretold by a whispering that surged along the shore, as the old women rustled words amongst them. So it was that Elka was warned of Tomas' forthcoming proposal. All things considered, it seemed to her a good thing; so she accepted, just as she had been told she would.

The weather turned on the Sunday, only a fortnight after the wedding. Though a fine grey rain now drove against the coast, the reek of baking fish from the kitchen was such that Elka saw fit to open the tall bay window that overlooked the quay. It was not long before a low mist began to gather in the room, but there she stood in the late of the morning, waiting for Tomas to wake and eat his lunch; watch the staccato tap of her forefinger against that cigarette. She had been warned about the chills that strike the bones and the diseases that eat at the lungs, but Elka was not one to be concerned about such feeble things as lungs or bones. Her brittle fingers cracked slightly as her left thumb swivelled the band on her left ring finger, and she looked on through the open window as the clouds started to drift inland.

It was a fine thing to be engaged to Tomas, she was always told. Yes, she replied, it is wonderful to be tied to those we love by marriage. No, the old women would chide; it is a wonderful thing to be married to a fisherman. Think of the fish! He could feed the five thousand, so great are his catches. This was also true, Elka thought. It was the nets, of course, those were his secret. Tomas knotted his own fishing nets, his ruddy fingers threading tight intricacies of rope as they sat together in the evenings. The lulling sound of no escape, that rustle-tug-rustle-tug of knot-tying, was one she hoped to become contented with as they sat together year after year. She caught a great gulp of sea air as she inhaled, for the window to the quay was still open.

The quay formed a bright crescent-moon set in the coast, strewn with flotsam, driftwood, spilled fish from the fishermen's catches, mealy crab shells. Anchored boats fanned from its curve, rising and falling with the rhythmic assurance that characterises the flow of blood about the body or of water against the shore. On a Sunday morning it was at rest, gulls squalling in the salt-stung air, and it was then that Elka used to walk, along the water's hem where its surge and suck veined the sand. She kicked the woven mounds of worms in the sand and felt the tug of the water beneath her feet as it tipped her forty-five degrees though she remained upright; was pulled out to sea though she walked straight ahead. Things have a habit of turning themselves on their head amidst such vastness, her father used to tell her. Try asking a man in the middle of the sea which way is forwards, which back; where he's come from and where he's going. But Tomas had seemed so very certain of his directions, and a man with his gaze fixed firmly on the horizon is an attractive prospect. Elka had watched him bringing in his catch, standing proudly on deck amidst a mass of glittering, slithering treasure he had dug from the waves. Elka fancied she had found her sea legs that day, for things seemed to shift and turn and dizzy her less: here, perhaps was safe harbour. Tomas did not complain, not with her sweet voice and blue eyes. It was said amongst some that Elka's having already crossed many seas in her short life made her quite a catch, a saying of which the boys at the quay did not tire for a long time. It was inevitably repeated in the wedding speeches, and Tomas had taken Elka's hand tightly in his beneath the table and they had laughed.

Elka had awoken at six. Already, darkness had lifted and given way to the dismal light that fell upon the days in this part of the world during the winter months, but she could see from the window that it was only a light fog that had crept inland and not the gnawing winds that sometimes sliced in against the coast. It would not be long before they set in, and on any other day it would have seemed a fine morning to stretch the legs. But there was plenty to be done indoors, for it was Sunday and the catch lay waiting for her on the kitchen table. By seven, she had halved, gutted and removed the skeleton of the two fine fish that had been carefully selected from last night's trawl. She did as she had been taught: hands sodden with oil, she smoothed herbs through their innards and, before placing the fish in the oven, chose a pointed knife and popped their eyes onto the kitchen floor, where they came to rest, quite forgotten.

Noon had drifted in with the clouds and Tomas awoke to eat his catch. Elka placed the dish in the centre of the table and, as she took a knife to its crisped scales, a small sigh of steam escaped its dainty pink flesh. Ah, Tomas exclaimed, such a fish! Such a catch! How he had struggled to reel it in for his Elka, and how beautifully she has prepared it for him! A great job between them, he thought, and rested his hand upon hers. Her fingers interlaced with his; two knotted hands. Her brightly cuticled nails tapped on the coarse skin briskly. What a dismal afternoon, she remarked, and rose to switch on the lights, erasing the shadows in the terse yellow glare. Stop pacing, Elka, come and eat, she was told. With a lowered gaze, Elka returned to the table, squinting in the harsh light.

The window had come off the latch and began to crash back and forth as strong gusts caught it. There would be a storm tonight, Tomas proclaimed, the wind was gathering strength. And what a catch there would be tomorrow, the fish churned to the surface by the storm! What a feast he would bring for his Elka to prepare! He shut the window firmly.

And what a storm there was that night. How the sea smashed against the quay, how soundly Tomas rested, knotting the sheets tightly about them, until Elka was feverish in her sleep. Sweat dripped into her eyes and ran into the corner of her mouth and she tasted salt. In the dense, sleep-sodden shadows she fancied that the storm had crept into her head and seeped from her eyes.

When Tomas returned the next evening, Elka felt something strike at her spine. A broad smile on his face, Tomas stood in the doorway in a posture of unadulterated triumph. It seemed the storm had indeed been good to him. For in his arms Tomas bore a tremendous, fleshy fish tail, its scales as wide as thumbnails. He dropped it on the kitchen table with a thump, and its tattered fin drooped over the ledge. Elka regarded it for a moment, before she took a knife and set about peeling the iridescent skin, thick as leather, from the plump flesh. As she did so, Tomas' arms knotted themselves tightly about her waist and he kissed her cheek firmly, as if something had at last been settled between them. He was ablaze with stories as she began the preparations. They had shared it between the two of them, such an almighty fish it was, and tangled in the nets no more than a few yards from the shore! The storm had brought it in, Tomas was sure, for a fish that size would only be found as far out at sea as the horizon was visible from the quay. How proud she was of her Tomas, she told him; how his hours of knotting and weaving those nets had paid off. Elka took the carving knife and sliced the tail down its length, prising it into two halves. She found herself staring at the pearly, sturdy skeletal structure. Was that viscera she glimpsed beneath the fillets? And muscle? Had it been dead when it was pulled in, she wondered? Oh no, Tomas replied, oh no, quite a fight. She could well imagine the power of that thrashing tail, its writhing, skeleton and muscle flexing, garrotted by the netting. What a man it must have taken to reel in a creature that strong, she told him. She was glad she did not have the head to deal with, for she could well imagine how its eyes had rolled and bulged. And with a pop they would have to land on the kitchen floor.

Throughout the afternoon the pungent scent of the baking fish tail grew steadily, and Tomas' eyes fairly gleamed. Its aroma was distinctive, no doubt because of its size; something akin to meat, didn't she agree? Yes, Elka certainly did. She had needed both hands to pull out its bones before baking, as she had been taught. A catch like no other, Tomas repeated, pouring another glass of whisky in anticipation. His hand clamped firmly over hers when she went to unfasten the latch of the bay window, for it was a sharp wind that had arrived since the storm, and Elka's cheeks were already aglow. He picked up her hand. See? She was shivering. Elka, not one for such feeble things as bones or lungs, found herself strangely weak at the knees, and her breath quite stopped. Was she feverish? Tomas laid his hand upon her forehead, and Elka was puzzled to notice that she recoiled. She would just go and stretch her legs before the meal, she reassured him; a walk down to the quay would clear her head. Tomas watched her figure descending the cliff path from the tall bay window.

It was not the sound of agitated water, nor of whispering, but it was nevertheless obvious to Elka that something had happened as she descended to the quay, for things have a way of making themselves known along the coast. Like gulls perched on rocks, the old women sat lined up on the benches leading down the cliff path. They glanced up and caught their breath sharply as they saw her. Johanna and Susannah stepped deftly before her, arms linked, eyes wide.

'On my dear, you can't go down to the quay, it's been closed off —'

'Closed off — ' Susannah echoed. Perhaps she caught a glimpse of Elka's eyes, for she reached out and touched her arm gently. 'And how is your Tomas?'

The nature of storms is one of turbulence. They upturn things settled firmly, draw in what is far out. The sea's surface is hurled aside like a blanket and its innards churn and swarm. Curious things we would never dream were there float to the surface and are tossed ashore, like a grand declaration of the unexpected. And so perhaps it's not so very strange that a woman should have been found washed ashore in the quay that morning after the storm — it is, after all, a dreadful but inescapable fact that people are lost to the sea every day.

But what induced the whispers was that not a woman, but half a woman was churned up on the shore. The naked torso ended at the line of her hips, a neat slice encrusted with salt crystals forming a dull sheen at the nape of the belly. There have been cases of sharks in these parts, she told herself. Somewhere, she repeated, there was a pair of legs drifting far from their owner. Old women talk utter nonsense, she told Tomas later as she toyed with her food over dinner. To say the storm should have pulled her out to sea! To say she was dragged ashore! It made her so angry, that was why she cried, that was why the salt stung her eyes! Tomas laid down his knife and fork, and held her, knotting her tightly in his arms.

Though Elka had always known things functioned in ways she couldn't be certain of along the coast, she soon came to realise that the sea was in fact a strange and illogical place; that it was better to leave it be than try to dredge up its secrets, or indeed truths. This was confirmed when, at the age of fifty, Tomas disappeared from the grey horizon at the point where the waves merge with the sky; where above or below, before or behind cease to have any meaning. With lungs full of salt-water and heavy fisherman's boots, he sank to the seabed, the pressure screeching in his ears until the drums burst. The sound was not unlike a screaming woman.

Elka, of course, knows nothing of this. How could she? She likes to say his end was a peaceful one; that he rests back with the treasures he once dug from the waves. She lives quietly in their house overlooking the quay, but no longer has to leave the tall bay window open, for there is no longer the reek of slowly roasting fish about the house. There are whispers, yes; but proposals have had the sense not to accompany them. She spends her days walking along the shore as she used to, and even indulges in the occasional swim. At night, with a deft kick of the legs, she hurls the sheets from the bed.

Automation

Ann Winter

Latex fingers lift my elbows and twist them out, pulling the skin tight and exposing my inner arms. One hand grips the elbow in a surgical vice, while the other strokes cool an ointment along the upturned veins. It courses through my nerves like a live current, then my arms go numb. 'We'll switch your headset on in a few minutes,' says a female voice, muted and distorted by the transmitters that propel it the distance from her mouth, through the computerised processors and into my earphones. 'How do you feel?'

'Fine.' I am terrified.

'We can hear you perfectly. Your heart rate is quite accelerated, but that's normal, it will slow down soon. If you want us to halt the program, speak into your microphone at any time.'

A pale electric haze filters across the screens in front of my eyes. All over my body my nerves sensitise and deaden, spreading from my arms up into my chest and neck, along my trunk, my pelvis, and into my legs. A high magnetic hum fills the pause, harmonising in my earphones with my soft, sedated pulse. The metallic voice buzzes again in my ear.

'Yesterday we talked about a dream.'

I am watching them rebuild our family from parts, like Airfix models. Large hands, so large the rest of their bodies are permanently out of view, are snapping individual arms and legs out of plastic frames and arranging them in classes of size and type. One grid contains arms and hands, separated into their microscopic components. The giant fingers line up every part in order of ascending size; left opposing right in crippled confrontation. I realise it's not just my family; it's my friends, my teachers, the doctor, our neighbours, our whole community disabled, waiting to be re-attached.

41

The hands break each limb off its stem with tweezers or gently pinched fingers, as if picking soft fruit. They leave the heads until last; hairy, unripe berries, hanging by the throat on a plastic branch.

Their work outgrows the table and soon even the room. Whenever two body parts are attached, they begin to swell and take on colour like living organisms. My head is heavy. I can't sleep, I feel as if I haven't slept for a week.

'Where is your mother?' asks the electronic nurse.

They start with my mother. They stick her arms together, then her legs. They turn the minute material with tweezers and tiny screwdrivers. They are so immersed they don't notice her arms and legs expanding. Then they panic and stick them on the nearest torso, but it's the doctor's! Too late! They are sticking anything anywhere; my teacher's right hand waves at the doctor's head stump, my brother's leg flails and kicks from my father's shoulder, my arms flounder back to front on our neighbour's twitching hips.

I watch them from the doorway of their abattoir of mannequins, stitching up their monstrous collages. Among the muddle I can easily recognise my father's arms and legs, growing, detached. The hands fight bravely against the nature of the material, adjusting and correcting, trying to force on it a sense of proportion. They remove my friends' heads from their plastic stems and attach them randomly to any neck, arm or leg stump facing towards me. The heads stare resentfully into the doorway, challenging and appealing.

Suddenly I am inside a headless, dislocated body. The atmosphere is tense and electric. Malign currents of energy radiate from the stultified joints and redundant limbs littering floor, each one frustrated by its isolation, and uselessness.

'Yesterday we also talked about your school.'

My school is small. It's a ten minute walk from home, past the steel plant. When I first start attending my mother gets us up at 7 a.m. and we cross the town on two buses to avoid the picketers outside the factory.

If the strike comes up on television or the radio we change the channel quickly and find some music. When music comes on my mother whirls me round the room gripping my arms tight, singing loudly and frightening me with her false gaiety. She spins me off my short legs, turning and twirling like a dervish until she is sure she has driven the strike from my mind.

Our town is famous but the reason is secret. The people who used to work inside the steel plant are now in the street, waiting.

'We are seeing the strike again. You know what we agreed. If this continues we'll have to turn the machine off. Try to concentrate on the school.'

      I'm walking to school with my father.

      'That's good.'

My father isn't going to work today, he's taking me to school. We're leaving much later than usual, and that must be why we're not walking to the bus stop. We're walking towards the steel plant, in silence.

I hear shouting and chanting. At the top of the hill, I look down and see hundreds of strikers swarming around the factory gates below us, carrying colourful signs and banners. They drift randomly like extras on a film set; directionless, awaiting instruction. My father strides down towards the picket, pulling me behind him. He's saying: 'Come on, step out! One foot in front of the other!'

I'm afraid. Fear rises in my throat, choking back responses. We are walking right into something whose name is banished in our home, and the nearer we come, the more anxious I feel.

The pictures are clearer than ever. The crowd ahead of us is parting like shooting sparks off a hot blade. A large grey Daimler and three black Mercedes are sliding soundlessly past, surrounded by police motorcycles. Behind them crawl four riot vans.

The protesters have been waiting for hours to witness this presidential cavalcade. As soon as it comes into sight they spring into action, pressing in around the vehicles, waving painted signs and shouting: 'Bankrief out!' or 'Bankrief's a thief!'

We are being caught up in the surge and squashed into the pack around the cars. My father is gripping my fist with one hand and poking and thumping furiously at the people around us with the other, shouting into the chanting: 'Bloody fools! There's a child here! Watch the child!' My cheeks are being crushed against a cartoon of a portly politician, picking the pockets of thin steelworkers. Then the board it's stuck to takes off, scraping past my face and soaring up into a patch of blue sky far above me. A chant is rippling across the crowds, gathering momentum like rolling thunder: 'Bankrief's a thief, he gives nothing but grief!'

Somehow my father has managed to pull us out of the crush and up towards the television cameras, where we can see the whole surrounding area. The demonstrators have closed off all our exits. Everyone is hungry for confrontation; a chance to show their mettle in a fair fight. The banners of different trade unions and pressure groups sway over the heads of the picketers, displaying their logos like battle standards, subduing the opposition with a shake of their strong, united fist.

My father's mood is darkening as we settle down to watch and wait. Placards change hands and new ones appear, their colourful faces following the vehicles like sunflowers raising their heads towards a rising sun.

The picture on the screen freezes. Then the still starts to roll in wide vertical lines, a dream pinched flat between two mangle rollers. I am coming out of a trance. The lights go on. The room around me is stark and unfamiliar.

I am preparing to speak, but before I can clear my throat two voices penetrate my earphones. They are extremely faint, but I can just make out their discussion.

'…should let her talk about it.'

'I'm sorry? Doctor –'

'We've been discouraging it throughout her treatment, with no success. She hasn't recovered any balance. She's still obsessive. Perhaps we should encourage her to give her obsession free reign; to get it out of her system.'

'Isn't that risking another breakdown?'

'In here?'

'She's regenerating some pretty charged images. Her stress levels are high.'

'I still think it's worth the risk. Let's see how far she will go with it. If we think she's becoming over-excited, stop the machine and I'll give her a sedative.'

There is a pause, in which I'm trying to distinguish what I've just heard from the snapshots and sensations of the past I've been immersed in. As I learn to breathe in water my head is yanked up into the air, and thrust under the surface again when my breathing returns to normal. Miraculously, the room goes dark and the screen flickers back into life. I inhale deeply. The picture is unfocused. The black and white dots look like the heads of a vast crowd filmed from a great height. They separate to allow the wide lines, then the picture to appear, like the demonstrators splitting before the employers' cars.

I can see the faces of the passengers in the vehicles. They are viewing the crowd with disinterest, trying to ignore the seething mass of bodies bellowing into the blustery weather beside them. Inside their big, soundproofed cars they hear only a low vibration, rumbling gently of discontent, while around them hundreds of mouths move in silent fury, closing and opening in exaggerated mime, as if shouting under water.

The cars pass into the plant, followed by the first riot van, which stops just inside the compound, while the other three drive onto the curb and park predatorily opposite the gates.
The doors of the first van fly open and a squad of armoured policemen spring out, gripping truncheons in one hand and riot shields in the other. They crouch in the entranceway, hunching against each other and slotting their shields together to form defensive wall.
As the motorcade is disappearing into the plant, the irrepressible crowd spills into the space it vacates; only to pause and retreat before the barricade of riot shields pushing menacingly towards them.

'Where are you and your father? We've lost sight of you. Have you found a way out? Have you made it to school?'

We can't go anywhere. There are too many people. We are forced to stay where we are and watch. The camera crews and news presenters soon retreat into their location vehicles. Over the heads of the picketers, time-worn green canvases flutter like the banners of a disinherited army, sheltering the leaflets and tea urns on the foldaway tables underneath.
Biting winds are pulling the damp, freezing air close around us, testing our nerve and their determination to hold out for the rally. People are pressing together for warmth, burrowing into layers of winter clothing. Near the tables, gloved hands are clutching polystyrene cups filled with hot liquid, each one sucked at jealously by the cold air, which whips up

a collective cloud of steam to condense on the drinkers' frozen faces.

'Where are you? Where is your father?'

He's watching me. We are next to the location vehicles, looking down at the crowd. A man with a long brown beard and a red bobble hat is laying out camera cables near our feet.

'Do the pictures go up those wires?' I am asking him.

'Of course, where else?' he laughs. 'They get all squashed and mixed up like scrambled eggs. There's a big room in the BBC where they sort through all those ears, mouths, eyes and noses when they come out of the wire, and stick them back together in time to go on TV.'

'What if they get lost?'

'They never get lost. But sometimes they make mistakes. Next time you're watching telly have a good look at the people's faces. Quite often they end up with the wrong nose, or with their eyes or ears back to front. Now you know the secret you'll be able to spot it.'

'Don't be daft!" laughs my father, bursting the bubble with characteristic rigour. "She's got a big enough imagination as it is, don't encourage it!" The man shrugs, but he's winking at me as he turns back to his work.

'How long do you expect them to hold out?' my father is asking him.

'A couple of days, a couple of weeks,' the sides of his mouth drag down, making his shoulders rise. 'If they reach a deal today, we can all go home.'

'If!' snorts my father, disgusted with everyone: the union, the government, and the demonstrators. They are exchanging views on the strike, while I am examining the kinks in the wire for the outlines of lost ears and noses. Then the picture goes blank, and the static haze returns.

'Try to relax,' the electronic voice fades into my earphones. 'You're breathing very fast. Take long, deep breaths.' The magnetic hum returns, but thankfully the room remains dark.

'Take a drink.' The lip of a glass or a mug is pushed against my lips and cold, sweet liquid spills over the edge. A cloth dabs and wipes briskly at my neck and chin. Then the voice fades, receding from the participatory sphere, retreating into the intimate hum of the programme controlling my automated memory.

Once again, the picture is dissolving into a mass of jumping smoke particles, popping and crackling across the screen. I blink and the doctor and his eager encouragers disappear.

I can see the police barricade opening to allow the motorcade through. The crowd is grinding into action, waving banners and placards, calling out chants, desperate for a response worthy of their long vigil. Their reflections are rolling off the polished bodywork of the cars like water running off glass. Once more the passengers pass them unmoved.

In their frustration, picketers are swarming into the path of the vehicles, inadvertently blocking the police in the gateway from the object of their protection.

Suddenly plastic batons are rising and falling mechanically on the heads and shoulders of people trapped by the crowds ahead of them, powerless to escape the assault.

Seeing their colleagues' predicament, the relief teams pour out of the riot vans and fall on the unarmed protesters in front of us, forcing their shields into the writhing jungle of arms and faces, hacking left and right with their truncheons, trying to clear a passage for their fellow officers. People break out of the crowd, screaming and cursing with pain. They stumble blindly towards us, eyes running with blood, blood pouring from cracked foreheads, lips and broken noses.

'Don't look!' orders my father. He picks me up and runs behind a van, trying to shield my eyes from the violence. I hide my face, shaking and screaming, expecting a baton to smash down on us any minute.

The crowd is writhing and scrambling against itself in anarchic chaos. In their panic, people are shoving and punching each other, pushing in conflicting directions. Some are using their cardboard signs to deflect the baton blows, or trying to return the attack. The majority are simply panicking.

Somewhere above the storm, the press cameras are rolling and flashing, until the police force the reporters into their vans and place a guard on them, ostensibly for their own protection.

'Do you want to take a break? Raise your fingers, or move your head for yes.'

I can't feel anything. I can't move. The possibility of movement is so remote I am not even sure if I'm trying.

'Let's continue then. Yesterday we talked a lot about your school friends. Can you visualise them outside the dream? What is it like at school?'

I have no particular friends. I am drifting sleepily around the playground, in and out of dizzy gangs of children, occasionally catching a ball or joining a game, then quickly dropping out and moving on alone. Now the strikers' children are standing beside me on the sidelines, watching through dreamy, half-closed eyes as other children play in the cavernous school yard. They stick to me aimlessly, like sleepwalkers stranded in someone else's dream. They are following me home. I find them floating in the dark hallway outside my room, swaying, tipping their feet up and arching into backward rolls, or plummeting into a dive as if buoyed up by water. At night we revel in our weightlessness, bouncing off walls and running across ceilings. We are a troupe of acrobatic astronauts, performing gravity-defying tricks in the air.

'Do you only see this at night? What about the day?'

I am at school, worn out, unable to concentrate or retain information. My mind is replaying the previous night. My lack of gravitation is weighing on my mind, making me sluggish and apathetic. The teacher's words are making little sense to me, and nothing corresponds to the reality of our town since the strikes failed. None of these classes are preparing us for the vast expanse of nothing we see ahead of us. There are career lessons, but there are no tutorials on mass unemployment or economic decline.

'Let's leave school now. Think about what you did outside school.'

I can't see it anymore. A dense purple cloud clings to all the town's buildings, disfiguring our homes, bruising the streets. The town is submerged in a fog of disaffection. Whenever it lifts for a few hours, a few more doors and windows have been bricked up. Visibility is poor and my life is slowing down to a cautionary crawl. We creep warily out of our houses and get lost in the treacherous murk, forgetting where we are going and what we are looking for. Those who find their way home are even more disorientated than before.

I can't remember what our town looked like without this heavy purple ceiling, filtering out the sun and leaving us in this perpetual violet twilight.

The insidious damp is playing havoc with our electricity, wetting wires and drizzling into sockets. Electrical fires flash and fizzle out in purple puddles as soon as the material ignites. The damp eats through clock faces and rusts up their metal arms, and I am quickly losing track of time. I am not thinking about the future. Prospects for employment are bleak, since the steel plant was automated. Some of us find jobs in the battery factory or the new call centre to the north of the town. The rest of us collect our benefit, and begin our endless wait for the world to change.

'Where are you now?'

I am trying to sleep. I am fifteen, I am sleeping in my clothes and shoes. I am waking up in a street half a mile from the house, or standing in the middle of the park at dawn, or in front of the school, or at the gates of the steel plant.

'Your records show you consulted a doctor about your insomnia. Can you picture the meeting? What is the surgery like?'

My mother and I are in a waiting room, forced back against the walls by the concentrated apathy emanating from the other patients. Loud, laborious breathing, amplified by surgical tubes, penetrates the dense atmosphere. The breaths are so voluble the room vibrates with each strangled inhalation. We all sit motionless, succumbing to the soporific sound.

The door swings open and the doctor springs in, with all the theatre of a cabaret compere. His black hair gleams with pomade and a jaunty red bow tie blooms at the collar of his white coat. He shakes each patient's hand, grinning maniacally. 'How's the incontinence, Mrs. Baddler?' He addresses the room, chuckling with exaggerated bonhomie, as if we all share a naughty secret. The old woman simpers, confused, and he pulls a face, as if surprised by unpleasant odours. 'And you, Mr. Torath, how's your gurgler? Your piping's rattling around like a loose exhaust!' The doctor shakes the old man's hand and instantly the loud breathing stops. The man's face reddens and he lets the hand drop. The breathing resumes. The doctor catches my eye, gives a big theatrical wink and flashes his showbiz smile. He skips across the room.

'You're new! What's up?' He leans towards me until his white coat settles on my knees. My tongue freezes.

'She doesn't sleep' breaks in my mother. 'Or at least, she sleepwalks. It's driving us mad. She's always done it. Honestly doctor, we can't get any rest.'

'I see.' The doctor frowns, suddenly serious. 'What's troubling you?' He studies me carefully.

'Nothing at all. Why would there be?' interrupts my mother again with a laugh, eyeing me sideways. 'She's doing fine. Perhaps it's her schoolwork.'

'Are you worried about your schoolwork?' The doctor looks at me searchingly. Suddenly my mouth opens and words rush out.

'The fog! It's all this fog!' I blurt, and then look around in surprise.

'The fog? What fig! The fog! What can she mean?'

'She's got such an imagination!' giggles my mother, coquettishly, 'really doctor, you should see the way we run around after her,' she gurgles. 'Quite literally, actually, it's not easy trying to find her in the morning. Her father drives round, scouring the streets and the parks... quite a job in this town.' The doctor's face relaxes into its habitual stage grin. He turns towards the other patients and thumbs back at me.

'Mummy and Daddy's little favourite, don't you know!' He crows. Everyone laughs.

'Absolutely. What a professional,' cries my mother, flirting outrageously. 'Thanks very much, Doctor, your diagnosis is spot on.'

'I can prescribe something for it,' calls the doctor, playing to his audience. 'Waste your life, drop out, go on the dole, go on the streets – that ought to cure their partiality.'

'She's beginning to respond to the program, not the stimulus.'

'What do you mean?'

'She's enjoying it, playing with the images, creating scenes, exaggerating gestures... these are conscious constructs, not memories.'

'Is this a sign of recovery? Or adaptability?'

'That's what I'm not sure of. She must be tired; that will alter the quality of her recollections too. Let's press on a little, go back to the strikes. We'll pull her off after five, that gives us another forty-five minutes.'

'When do you see the strikers again?'

Their faces are incorporated into my nightmares. Every night, blood encrusted eyes, mouths, T-shirts, jeans, trainers stained red-brown. The strikers lurk in the dark streets outside looking for a way into our home.

'Does anyone protect you?'

My mother stands in the driveway dressed in plated armour. She is indomitable proof against truncheons and strikers alike, guarding the house from attack.
I am troubled by her lack of a horse and standard, return to my room to find them. When I come back, minutes, days, weeks later, her helmet is lying on the ground beside her feet, with her head in it. Next, both strikers and the armour disappears. Her head is back in place. She kneels on the driveway in the dark, with her eyes closed and her hands pressed in prayer.

'Think about the town. What happens to the strikers now?'

The fighting is a pretext for the employers to fire anyone who has been on strike. The picket shrinks to a few solitary men. My mother, my brother and I hurry past them in the mornings on our way to school.

Every day we see busloads of replacement workers from other towns being driven into the plant. The strike breakers cover their heads, trying to block out the cry of bitter fury ('Scabs!') that seeps in through the cracks in the rattling window frames.

The news is moving on, and the protesters drift despondently back home, to take their places within the crisis of unemployment that is engulfing the community.

Photographs are still appearing in the local press showing police brutality against unarmed strikers and the injuries the latter sustained. But nationally the story is tossed on the slag heap of yesterday's news, to be picked over occasionally for coke to smoulder in the Sunday supplements. The workers have bared their muscle power, and been shown the reflection of their own impotence.

The plant rumbles back into action. A hostile rift bursts open in the town between those who return to work and the majority, who either refuse or are unwelcome. Hundreds drift along on unemployment benefit, haunting the town like a phantom strike; sad, involuntary parasites sucking away at its ambience until the place becomes visibly drained, drab and dispirited.

Far from being an isolated case, my condition becomes the norm. The whole town is populated by sleepwalkers, trapped in the widening fissure between memory, imagination and reality.

'Yesterday we talked about you leaving school.'

I am sixteen, when I leave school. I see no point in staying on. I sign on automatically. Besides the call centres and out of town superstores, the single growth industry in our town is recreational drugs, demanding or supplying, never both. Brokering broken dreams is a highly competitive career. My role in the burgeoning black economy is strictly supportive: reinvesting the taxpayers' money in the tools to evade the realities the government has created.

'You haven't mentioned the fog. Has it gone? Are you seeing more clearly now?'

No. Now the purple fog is spreading far beyond our town, but here it is thickest, seeping into homes through cracks in the doors and windows. The dense mist is saturating everything, weighing down fabric and flesh and fuddling our brains. It's vaporous, even viscous in places. Energy currents are warping through it, animating and shaping clouds which are clustering and moulding themselves into intricate patterns or words before bursting and reforming into familiar faces, or silhouettes I recognise. The mist is intelligent matter. It is revealing to me its powers of manifestation. I am sharing its wisdom freely, spreading its gauzy messages around town.

I carry cans of purple spray paint everywhere. The haze is forming its fuzzy images I am copying them onto any available surface. I am starting with the trees and walls in the park and graduating to the boarded up doors and windows. It is the second wave of strikes and there are more union slogans everywhere. Picketers are paying me to spray words on the plant and the managers' cars.

'Can you picture this second wave of strikes? What's happening? We can see the employers at the plant again.'

A crowd is gathering behind the cordons opposite the plant entrance, watching a line of sleek black Mercedes slide through the gates. This time they are escorted by television vans, instead of riot police. The employers are back. We all listen to the Secretary for Trade and Industry read out an emotive speech, praising the plant as the most efficient producer of steel in the country. Then we watch it all again on television. He is declaring the steel plant's automation an unqualified success. The employers' foresight is duly applauded.

In London, the prime minister announces plans to privatise the entire steel industry. Her speech is peppered with American euphemisms, sanitised by their sporty, scientific meanings: 'Streamlining', 'Performance Enhancing', 'Downsizing'. Four steel plants are earmarked for immediate closure.

Although its presence at the plant is greatly diminished, the union strikes in sympathy with those affected by the closures. In the violet fog bank surrounding the compound, two battered canvases flap dismally over the heads of a twenty-man picket, more like deserted rags on an abandoned battlefield than the flags of a rebel army. Placards and banners hang shapeless and indistinct on the gateposts, too numerous for the men to carry. Those not protected with plastic are turning to mulberry mush in the rain. The banners sag with the weight of the water, hanging limply on the railings like used bandages.

Picketers with clip boards are weaving among the cars at the new traffic lights outside the plant, collecting signatures for petitions and donations for the strikers. Cars are slipping past and being replaced seconds later by identical rows of tired drivers, commuting home. The road is like a giant treadmill, pulling interchangeable vehicles through the low, murky sky. They ask the same questions, air the same resentments, and repeat the same arguments.

'Why bother to strike? The unions have no power.'

'Steel production will be sold to anyone, sold abroad, and who will we be fighting then? Pension scheme investors? We must act now.'

'Join us, strike with us.'

'A lot of good you did us ten years ago. Look at us now.'

Ten days later the strikes are called off. There is no-one to confront. At best the employers see steelworkers as a resource, to be redeployed elsewhere, or at worst, as old-fashioned, uneconomical material to be dumped in the interests of increased productivity.

Once the strikes are over the protesters in our town return to their jobs. No immediate disciplinary action is taken. Meanwhile the five plants chosen for closure begin to wind down production. More towns are thrown into depression. Scabs stand in dole queues beside seasoned picketers. Steelworkers haunt the streets of all our dismal towns, suspended in the fickle moment of release, like the shells of the liquidated steel plants: stripped, pending ultimate resolution.

I spray paint their foggy shapes all over town. I stop thinking about where the paint is falling. I spray across the pictures, furniture, clothes and wallpaper in my parents' and friends' houses. I am eighteen. I am painting shapes on a bus-stop shelter. I spray over three people in the queue, getting a man who tried to stop me in the eye.

'What happens to the man? In the picture he's on the ground. Is he seriously harmed? Does he recover?'

I am being arrested for vandalism, assault and grievous bodily harm. I am feeling no remorse. I don't think he's hurt, but the police say I have blinded him. They're insisting I'm dangerous, they're saying I'm insane. I am disorientated, the pictures are spinning, I might be asleep or awake. I may be hallucinating. Neither the detectives, the psychologists nor the lawyers have heard of the purple fog, although it has been darkening the town since I was at school. My friends all testify. Their statements say I speak about the fog often. They think it sounds funny, or cool, but they do not know what it means.

'You blinded a man with an aerosol spray. I can confirm that. We have the records of your arrest here. Do you still feel no remorse?'

How can I answer? The pictures are in front of me, plain and senseless as the nose on my face. There he is, reeling about on the pavement, being stretchered away into an ambulance. I am sorry for hurting him. I never knew I could.

'Let's look at the strikes from another angle. Your father works in the privatised plant, in the administration department. He has a good salary, company shares and a private pension scheme. None of that would be possible if the strikers had won.'

It's prize giving at school: I am being presented with a badge for a group geography assignment. My parents are smiling proudly. 'We didn't do such a bad job on you!' they say, as if the credit for my badge is really theirs. I feel remorse but it's hard to say what for.

'We are closing down the program. In a few moments, the screens will go blank.'

In the dark my nerves tingle. Vaguely I sense my numbed limbs being touched, massaged, lifted, dropped. They are detaching me from the machine. Remorse overwhelms me.

'Her visual responses have been exemplary, we're very excited about this treatment,' says the doctor's voice. 'She distinguishes clearly between images formed during sleep and conscious input, she has successfully identified fact, differentiated from fantasy. She has completed her rehabilitation program. We do not anticipate any recurrence of the illness which led to her internment.'

'Will she be able to work?' asks a voice that sounds like my father's.

'There is no reason why she cannot function as any normal member of society,' the doctor is saying.

'How wonderful! A normal member of society! Clever girl!' calls another voice, which must be my mother.

'There is one thing. We've realised now that it is important for her to talk about the strikes. I know this contradicts everything we've said before, but we now believe it is quite safe to encourage this. Try treating it as a hobby, a personal interest in local history. Perhaps she could research the disputes in the local library, read a few books and old papers, that kind of thing. It's not a good idea to bury it.'

The voices go on and on, tidal sound washing towards and away from me in the blackness.

'Why talk about the strikes?' asks my father, addressing me. 'Everything's so much better now, better than you remember. The strikers ruined this town, not the government. If they had gone quietly, less people would have suffered.'
    'But –'
    'Your father's right. You'll see, when we get back into town,' my mother chips in, her voice rising excitedly. 'There are new shops and restaurants, and a lovely café where we can have tapas, or lattes, or pain au chocolat. Would you like that?' I see myself nod glumly, feeling the milky white foam clogging up my throat. We are in the car, driving away from the hospital. They pass the rest of the journey in satisfied silence.
    My parents are quizzing me about my ambitions and interests. They are showing me an application form for a filing job in the administration department of the steel plant. They are helping me complete it, and showing me where to sign.

Twenty years later the streets around Westminster are pounding again with stamping protest marches. Each one seems unconnected with the rest. Popular dissent is alive but mixed up like the unstuck bodies in the dream. It trumpets smug convictions without the power to convince itself. Demonstrators fall on Westminster in their thousands, but on the television screen their actions seem simply cathartic, even carnivalesque. The government sits tight and waits for the squall to pass.

Somewhere amid the uproar, Fortress Group Plc., the owner of what remains of the steel corporation, is announcing the closure of our steel plant. Unwise foreign investments have caused serious financial losses for the company, which now have to be redressed by large-scale downsizing. Within a week, union membership at the plant triples. The workers are grasping at reeds for rafts of buoyancy to keep their heads above water. In the intervening decade, the union has learned much from observing the new economic climate and the way other lobby groups and public bodies have kept themselves afloat. A delegation of negotiators meet sympathetic government ministers, and with their support, present the board of executives with a bid to buy the plant, on behalf of a co-operative formed by the employees themselves.

One wet afternoon in March, the press return to the plant for the third time in twenty years. This time, we are standing on the other side of the picket, huddled under a makeshift shelter by the gates. Ten of us are manning the picket, eight others plus my father and I. Professionally printed signs lean against the table and the backs of our chairs, far too many for us to carry.

Traffic from the town slips by, drivers and passengers glancing at us indifferently. We are part of an interminable intermediate, all images and slogans, suppressed between their departure points and final destinations. We are hardly looking at the passing cars. We aren't collecting donations, the union is subsidising the strike. We are registering our dismay, our sense of betrayal. We are showing ourselves as the human cost of bad business: pleading for charity from who knows who. We are still standing, resigned to our final disinheritance and taking it with dignity. We are exhibits in a living museum, patiently presenting our futile testimony to posterity.

Fortress Group's board of executives reject the union's offer outright. Which hegemonic industry in its right mind would willingly foster its own competition? Arguments about the social and economical costs fall on deaf ears. Worse still, the government is backing the union's deal, exposing a facile weakness in its economic politics. Its authority was sold to the commercial sector long ago.

The chairman receives the union's offer with some show of pity. Still, he makes no attempt to conceal his unfortunate investment decisions. It's accepted as an inevitable risk. He feels no responsibility for his employees. The union is irrelevant. Somewhere, among the pistons and pulleys, the strong-arm might of British industry is stumbling around like an angry giant awakened from a three hundred-year sleep; finding itself betrayed by a reality altered beyond recognition, and blinded by the smokescreens of technocracy.

The chairman is freely acknowledging himself powerless. The decisions aren't his to make. He is hypnotised by the numbers passing continually in and out of his possession, multiplying, dividing, inexplicably vanishing. The numbers are controlling his decisions, each a mechanical assessment of profit and loss. The bigger the numbers grow, the more powerful Fortress Group becomes. The company is not the people, the buildings or the product. It is these swelling, shrinking, pulsating figures, writhing behind his screen like tiny larvae, each with a unique mating pattern. His job is to stabilise the delicate environment behind the screen, to secure optimum breeding conditions.

I thought they had switched the machine off, but the pictures keep flashing across the screen. Though the voices have gone.

Twenty-four years after that first strike, the gates of the plant are closing for the last time. The site is scheduled for demolition, but the process is being forestalled by the actions of local and national heritage groups, who are lobbying for the preservation of the Victorian administration block. Among the proposals for their redevelopment are: a living museum of the steel manufacturing industry; local history museum; a heritage centre with a theatre, cinema, café and conference rooms, and an art gallery for local artists.

The future is tourism, and each suggestion proposes hiring ex-plant workers. They will simulate their former jobs, demonstrating to visitors how the manual labour was done; or give guided public tours, explaining how the plant formerly functioned. In the gallery and heritage centre there will be plenty of opportunities for security guards, cloakroom attendants, cleaners, or catering staff.

My father and I remain outside the plant until the day it closes for good. We are the first exhibits in the newly championed public space. We blend easily into the landscape, until the day the plant slips behind the smokescreen of history and re-emerges, as a walk-in memory machine, a living museum. That day we suddenly become noticeable by our absence.

Painless

Mandy Sutter

The first time she saw him, he breathed fire.

It was a bright spring day. He had come to talk to her students about job opportunities. At the end of his talk, he took off his jacket and tie, rolled up his shirtsleeves and produced two long sticks with cloth wrapped round the ends, like giant matchsticks. Next came an old orange squash bottle full of clear fluid. He doused the end of the matches in the fluid.

'Anyone got a light?' he asked casually.

Trevor Sykes, from his perch in the back row, lobbed him one. And before the sentence about fire regulations had even formed on her lips, he'd swigged out of the bottle, lit the giant matches, put his mouth to one of them and blown a tongue of flame five feet long across her desk. Trevor Sykes swallowed his gum.

'Shit, miss. Can he DO that?'

'If you're lucky enough to be invited for a job interview,' he said to the class when he left, petrol still glistening on his chin, 'be sure to make an impact. As I did this afternoon.'

Later, when she wrote on the whiteboard, her marker pen juddered over bobbled patches.

He rang her a week after his talk to ask whether he'd left a book behind. *One Hundred and One Tricks*. It was there, a great fat thing, wedged behind a radiator. She opened it and read a paragraph about how everyone loves to be tricked, as long as it's done with charm. She laughed.

He suggested a pub on the Ring Road. It was one she had visited before and disliked, for having no character. She drank a large glass of red wine that shone like a traffic light. Sitting next to a fake coal fire, they talked about life. He talked about his job and a recent investment he'd made on the stock market. She talked about her difficulties with relationships; how she always seemed to feel too much and how it put men off. He suggested dinner.

They drove to an Indian restaurant on the outskirts of town. They sat in front of plates of bright red chicken. He cracked a few jokes. But the table was too big, the tablecloth a tiring white expanse between them.

'Time for home,' she said, without waiting for the dessert menu.

'Oh, that's a shame,' he said, and she saw something in his eyes. 'So you don't want to see me spinning plates, then?'

She followed him in her car for ages, twisting and turning down narrow country roads. They ended up at a small cottage in a row of similar ones. Inside, it was tidy and anonymous. He took off his shoes, revealing bright white socks. She watched him balance two big white plates on long sticks. A series of tiny movements with his wrists and they spun like flying saucers.

'You try,' he said, 'with just the one.'

'Me?' she said, 'I couldn't!'

But he insisted. He stood behind her, his arm under hers, his palm under her wrist. The warmth of his chest at her back.

'Relax,' he said. 'Relax your hand and let me do it.'

But her hand was stiff and her movements jerky, and the plate toppled and fell, bouncing on the carpet.

'I should go,' she said. 'I've got work in the morning.'

'One more try. Let your hand go into neutral.'

He pivoted her wrist and the plate stayed up.

'Oh!' she said, 'I'm doing it!' She leant into him, breathing his odour of soap and mint.

He gave her directions back. It wasn't as complicated as she'd thought.

Next time she saw him, she chose her outfit more carefully. Black velvet trousers and a red lacy top that showed black bra underneath.

She drank red wine again. Ice turned his Pernod white and cloudy. Their conversation was more animated than before. She laughed at his jokes, getting used to them.

'Let's skip the meal,' he said. 'I want to show you something.'

Back at his house, he was upstairs for so long that she went to the foot of the stairs and called.

'Don't worry,' he shouted, 'all will be revealed.'

He came down carrying a large roll of industrial-looking

plastic and a thick sack full of something heavy. His hair was dusty.

'I had to go up in the attic,' he said.

He unrolled the plastic into a dull runway on the deep pile carpet. Then he upended the sack onto it. Out pattered a rain of broken glass. It was probably ordinary glass, but in the warm light it looked like jewels; emerald; diamond; sapphire; ruby. She was breathless at such wealth.

He spread the glass on the plastic, making a glittering, spiky path. He took off his shoes and socks and rolled up his trouser legs. His calves were pale and hairy. He stood poised at one end of the sparkling landscape and held out his arms like a ballerina. Then he put his right foot on the glass and with a careful, rolling motion, transferred his weight slowly onto it. There was a crunching noise as the pieces moved against each other. She winced. His left foot hovered over the glass. Then he put it down and stepped onto it. Again, that squeaky crunching, like a small animal being crushed. She wanted him to stop but dared not speak in case it distracted him. The glass was real, alright - she could see edges everywhere, glinting in the lamplight.

But there was no blood. Or pain. He was still smiling. And going on, one foot steadily in front of the other.

'Watch this,' he said. And he lowered himself to a crouching position and sat down, ever so gently, on the glass. He took his shirt off, and tossed it onto the couch. His chest was pale, like his calves. He unfurled himself gradually until he was lying completely horizontal.

'Come to the side here. Hold my hands. Yes, both of them. Now, put your left foot on my chest. You can do it without standing on the glass. No, don't ask why. Just do it. That's right. Now, give me your weight.'

'What? You must be mad! You don't know how much I weigh!'

She tried to pull away but he held on to her hands.

'It's alright,' he said. 'I won't break.'

Her hands were sweating now. They felt slippery in his.

'What if I break one of your ribs?

'Your weight isn't what's important. Trust me.'

She stood there, swaying. He held her eyes, willing her on. His sureness was catching. A low excitement began to replace her fear. Hardly breathing, and in the tiniest of increments, she gave him her weight. She searched his face for the slightest change of expression, the minutest evidence of pain. But he smiled on, even when she lifted her right foot clear of the ground. She stood on his chest with her knees bent like a skier. Their eyes were locked. Their hands were pressed together. She felt his pulse in her palm, his warmth in the soles of her feet. It was like making a circuit.

They dismantled themselves carefully. 'Your turn,' he said.

'Me! What, me? You're joking. I couldn't possibly –'

'As long as the glass is in a good thick layer, the pieces shift for you. It doesn't hurt at all.'

It was all very well for him, she thought. She was different. The trick or the magic or whatever it was, wouldn't transfer. She was too heavy. Too soft. Her feet were too sensitive. But he took her hand and led her to the start of the sparkly way.

'It's alright,' he said. 'I'm here.'

Hardly believing that she was doing it, she put her right foot on the glass. It wasn't as sharp as she'd feared. But on the other hand, she didn't want to walk on it. She imagined a dagger shaped piece penetrating her instep. She felt faint.

'I'm here,' he insisted again. 'I won't let go.'

She closed her eyes, gripped his hand and stepped onto her right foot, waiting for the pain. It didn't come. She turned to him with wide eyes. He beamed.

'You see!' he said. 'It's completely painless. It's just a question of mind over matter.'

She went across, hanging onto him without reservation. He was right. As long as she trod carefully and slowly, the glass made way. It wasn't comfortable but it wasn't painful. It was like walking barefoot over a pebbly beach.

'Do you want to go back across?' he asked, but she shook her head. He brushed a piece of glass gently from the sole of her foot.

'This is the most important bit,' he said. 'Not letting any stray bits stick to your feet. You'll tread on them and really hurt yourself.'

It felt strange to let go of him and walk unaided to the sofa. She watched him sweep up the glass and pour it back into its thick plastic sack, then roll up the plastic sheet. He put the things out in the hall, and the living room seemed normal again.

But when he came back in, she realised that her blood had changed. It had started to grow and pulse at the sight of him. He was ready to show her a different trick, something with a pound coin.

'No more magic,' she said, and pulled him down onto the sofa.

When she woke the next morning, he wasn't in the bed. She sat up and looked around the room. It was bare, furnished in white melamine. A chest of drawers had a polite lace doily on top and the windowsill, three equally-spaced ornaments. It had the feel of a spare room. She smelt coffee. She unhooked a snowy towelling dressing gown from the back of the door, and went downstairs.

He was in the kitchen. He smiled as she came in.

'Coffee?' he said. 'Croissants?'

He opened the shining white oven door. They sat on tall pine stools to eat.

After breakfast, she went round the house putting on her clothes as she found them: knickers, bra, velvet trousers, red lacy top.

'Will I see you again?' she asked, as they stood on the doorstep. It was another fresh spring morning, and the garden was full of daffodils.

'Oh yes,' he said. 'Of course. Yes.'

She never saw him again. The evening he rang to explain, she had come in from work and was pouring herself a glass of red wine.

'I'm really sorry. I'm married. I took you to our holiday cottage. I know I should have told you, but I didn't want to spoil the magic of the moment.'

'I see,' she said.

She put the phone down and waited for the pain. She waited for the piercing, slicing feeling of rejection, that she'd experienced so often over the years. But it didn't come. She thought she must be having a delayed reaction and drank her glass of wine straight off to brace herself. She waited. But still, the pain didn't come. She paced up and down her sitting room, unable to believe it. She looked at the soles of her feet. They were smooth and clean. She examined her face in the mirror above the fireplace. It was true. There was no trace of pain anywhere.

The Big Drift

Thomas Fletcher

The lurid, green words 'NEXT GENERATION' are bubbled over the dirty pale wall of the wet and concrete subway that I walk through on my way to the bus station. Behind the words are the silhouettes of two doves, each with an olive branch hanging limply from their sharp beaks. Somebody has taken a black marker pen and looped the word 'Saddam' all over the green. And, in red, 'The Authorities Stole my Spaceship'.

The subway is dark and wet. My daughter and her friend recently found a man in here, sitting against the wall. His tongue was on the floor next to him. It had been cut out. They rang an ambulance, and the man went to hospital. A man lying in a hospital bed, trying to touch his teeth with the remains of his tongue.

I live with just my son now. My son went to University to study economics, but left at the beginning of his third year and came back. My daughter has left home. My wife left too, a long time ago. I am in my early sixties now.

I always wanted to be an astronaut. It started with a photo I saw in the Seventies, taken from one hundred and sixty miles above the surface of the Earth, of the Pacific Ocean. The ocean, in the photo, is half covered with a layer of strato-cumulus clouds, and the rest of the water is lit bronze by the sun and looks like a metal desert. The cloud hangs four thousand feet above the water, but in the photo it looks like the cloud and the ocean are almost touching. The photo now hangs on the wall at home, and I used to point at it and say to my daughter – before she moved away – 'Distance. That black scratch between the cloud and the water is four thousand feet thick. That's what distance does.'

And she would say, 'I know, Dad. Four thousand feet. I know.'

And I ended up teaching physics at a secondary school in Wakefield. The walls of my classroom were covered in photos of the moon, of the astronauts on their ways to and from the moon, of space-walks, of space debris, of the shadows of astronauts against the dust on the moon. My son listens to bands with names like The Bled, It Dies Today.

★   ★

My daughter was only staying with me for a few days when she found the man in the subway, because there was a concert in Leeds that she wanted to go to. This was just before Christmas. She was actually on her way back, on her way back from the train station when she found the man. My daughter and her friend went with him, in the ambulance, to the hospital, because they wanted to know what was going to happen to him. They were both quite upset, understandably. It's not the kind of thing you expect to find. It's the kind of place where a rape or a mugging might be expected, but a man with his tongue cut out?

★   ★

There is no sound on the moon, because there is no atmosphere that can be beaten into sound waves. For the same reason, there is very little colour – there is no atmosphere to refract the light from the sun, which means that just about everything is black or white or grey. (I imagine living on the moon to be like living in *Eraserhead* by David Lynch.) This lack of colour makes judging distances very difficult.

I am on a bus now, heading through the town. The windows of most of the buses in Wakefield are faintly rose-tinted, or maybe it's the air, some strange colour in the atmosphere. It is cold outside. It is February. I like the cold.

I like the music that Alice, my daughter, used to listen to when she lived with me. I don't know the names of the bands and singers that she liked, but the music was strange, orchestral, delicate, with vocals that sounded like somebody whispering, or distant telephone calls, or the ghosts of astronauts. I used to sit in her room with her sometimes, if she was upset about something, or if she wanted some help with her homework, and I would listen to her music, and I would like it.

I took the telescope that Alice bought me for my birthday, and pointed it at the moon, but the moon looked smaller with the telescope than without. I looked at the thing and realised that I was looking through the wrong end.

How could I be so stupid? I thought. *I know how to use a telescope.*

So I spun it round and looked through the correct end, but the moon still looked tiny and far away. I realised that I was looking through the wrong end again.

I kept trying, and failing, to look through the correct end of the telescope, but I couldn't find it, and the moon just got smaller and smaller, and in the end I just went to bed, confused and worried.

Once, in a class at school, a long time ago, before my children went to university, before my daughter left home, a pupil said to me, 'Sir, I read that when the universe stops expanding, the gravity of everything in it will pull it all back together again and that's how it will end.'

I didn't say anything at first. I just took off my glasses and put them on the desk and looked past him at a photograph on the back wall. The photograph was of Edward White space-walking, but most of the photo was occupied with a long, golden tube that connected White's spacesuit to the Gemini spacecraft. The tube was like some kind of umbilical cord, turning space into some huge, cold womb, or it was like his intestines had escaped and uncoiled, floating and writhing in a swimming pool, or in the bath, or in a canal.

'No,' I said.

'No?' he asked, 'No what?'

'No. I don't think that that is going to happen.'

'Why not?'

'Because the universe doesn't contain enough mass to generate the massive gravitational force that would be required.'

'How do you know?'

'I just don't think it's possible.'

'So what will happen?'

'I imagine that everything will continue to appear to drift apart as it appears to be doing at the moment.'

'Oh right,' he said. There was silence for a moment, and then he said, 'So how will it end?'

'I don't think it will,' I said, 'I think that it will go on forever.'

'What do you mean?'

'I mean that it won't ever end. It doesn't have to end.' There was another momentary silence. *'Forget about endings,'* I said, *'and if that confuses you, stop reading novels.'*

'I like reading,' he said. I didn't say anything. *'Goodbye Sir,'* he said.

'Goodbye Graham,' I said. *He left the room, and I sat at my desk for a while, looking at my photographs. My head filled with cold, stony, lonely solar systems.*

Siobhan and I got married relatively young, and we were happy for a while. A couple of decades maybe. We got married on New Year's Day, which we thought would be nice. All I can remember is the cold. We never argued. Even towards the end, we never argued. We just 'grew apart', according to her. Our conversations, interactions of any kind, were punctuated by longer and longer silences, pauses, absences, rests. I remember saying, 'I think we're drifting.'

'No,' she said, 'that implies that it's our choice.'

'Well,' I said.

'We're growing apart,' she said.

Drifting. Drifting was a more appropriate word, I think.

She said other things. One of the last things she said to me was, 'You're missing something. There's something you don't have that you should have.'

'What?' I asked.

'I don't know,' she said. 'I can't put my finger on it. But it wears me out. You don't mean to do it, but you drain me. You're a black hole. You need something, and I think I try to give it to you, subconsciously, and you just absorb it. And it disappears. You're very grey.'

'I don't know what you mean,' I said.

'You're very grey. You're bloodless. My colour bleeds into you to fill you up, to flood your veins, and it just disappears.'

'Oh,' I said. 'Oh.' This hurt me. All of this hurt me very much. 'You're talking about a vacuum,' I said.

'Yes,' she said, 'a vampire.'

'No. A vacuum.'

'I heard you,' she said. 'A vacuum. Yes. You're like a vampire. And I bleed into you. And I become like you. See. And I have to go.'

A vacuum. We never argued, but she was never afraid of hurting me. That was just her. She always used to say, 'We all have to suffer for the truth.'

And I always imagined that 'truth' would have a capital 'T', but now I wonder. We all have to suffer for the truth. That was one of the things that she used to say.

I tried to look at the moon through my telescope again the other night, but this time I looked through it and saw just this huge eye looking back, and it took me a while to realise that I was just looking at me. I spun it round, and looked through the wrong end, and it was still just me, but further away, just this eye, drifting further and further away, down the tunnel, into the vacuum.

And how can a telescope malfunction like this, just light and mirrors and glass and light?

And now, I'm going to see Siobhan. I saw her for the first time in years about two months ago, at the market in Barnsley. I saw her at the fishmonger's stall. I was behind her in the queue, and didn't realise it was her. She'd put weight on. I didn't realise that it was her until I caught a scent, a taste, that I recognised from over fifteen years ago, and then suddenly I knew that it was her. There was suddenly no way that it could not be her. 'Hello Siobhan,' I said.

'Patrick?' She turned around. I smiled at her. 'Jesus Christ,' she said, 'Patrick!' And she hugged me.

'Siobhan,' I said, 'how have you been? Where have you been hiding?'

'I haven't been hiding,' she said, 'I moved away. I guess I never told you.'

I was trying not to be angry with her for not telling the children, at least. I was trying not to be angry. I was trying not to let her know that I was angry.

We went to some place she knew. It was nice. I bought drinks. We talked for a while, and then I said, 'Have you missed me?'

'No,' she said, 'you were never there.'

'I was never where?'

'When we were together. You were never a presence. You were an absence. I couldn't miss you.'

'Oh,' I said. 'Oh. Maybe that was just compared to you.' I said that because I was desperate. I don't know why, but I needed her, so I tried to ignore the hurt and just flatter her. 'We were happy,' I said, 'I think maybe you had expectations that were too high. We were happy.'

'You were happy.'

'We were happy.'

'You were happy.'

'Were you not happy?'

'No.' There was a long pause. 'I'm happy now.'

'I'm not.'

'You know,' she says, 'you maybe weren't. Even when we were together. You maybe weren't.'

Eugene Cernan's photographic composite of the Taurus-Littrow valley flooded my mind. He was an astronaut on the Apollo 17 mission. I don't know why the thing entered my head at that point, but suddenly all I could think about was the vast, grey landscape against an absolutely black sky, the astronaut Harrison Schmitt small and white in the distance.

'You're happy now?'

'Yes. I've re-married.'

'Oh. What's his name?'

'Neil.'

'Neil?

'Yes. He knows I'm here with you.' She gestures to her mobile phone, lying flatly on the table. 'I texted while you were buying the drinks.'

'You know,' I said, 'I never even thought of looking for somebody else.'

'That doesn't surprise me.'

Astronauts that get to go to the moon reportedly live with depression forever afterwards, because they are led to believe beforehand that there is nothing more important to achieve.

'Any astronaut that goes to the moon suffers from depression forever afterwards because they feel like they'll never do anything as incredible again,' I said.

'Well,' she said, 'they probably never will. Is this relevant?'

'I'm not an *absence*,' I said, 'I'm not an absence at all. I never was. You just never understood me. There was a distance. There was a space between us. And we let it grow. We *drifted*. We could have prevented it. We could have stayed together. We could still get back together, Siobhan.'

'Patrick,' she said, standing up, '*move on*. That's what you can't do. You miss some opportunity, you fail at something, you lose somebody, and it stays with you, and you've just got this big mass of *nothings* inside you, and you suck it out of other people. You have to let things go. You have to set yourself new sights. Move on. I've remarried. I'm happy.'

'Siobhan,' I said, 'don't go. I want to talk with you some more.'

'You should see somebody, Patrick.'

'See somebody? Why?'

'Because you're not happy. You never were. You thought you were happy, but you weren't.'

'And what? Not being happy means that I'm ill? That I need help? There's something wrong with being unhappy now?'

'Hm. There's something wrong with you.'

'Siobhan, don't go. I want to talk with you some more.'

'You don't want to talk with me. You just want somebody to be silent with. You're just one big silence.'

'That's not even slightly true.'

'It's true or it's false. There is no 'slightly true'. And it's true. You just want somebody to fucking, to fucking spin around in space with. And all you've ever known is me. You just want somebody to occupy you because you're not there.'

And then she left.

That night there was a message on my answering machine from Alice. She was asking if she could stay with me for a few days. I rang her back immediately to say yes, but there was no answer, so I left a message on her answering machine, and I imagined my voice emanating from her telephone, just a voice in a dark house, or on the moon, just a disembodied voice, 'Yes. Yes of course you can stay with me. I'd like that,' just drifting through the dust, through the valleys, over Neil Armstrong's footprint.

I remember waking up one night, years ago, and I found tiny little astronauts exploring my hand, taking skin samples and measurements, the width of my fingernails, the height of a wart. Mapping my fingerprints. They seemed to be enjoying my low gravity. I silently urged them to take off their helmets, to try and breathe the nothingness that surrounded me, to know true silence, devoid of their intercoms, to curl up and die, to adorn my dusty body with their tiny human corpses.

★   ★

My daughter and her friend – Janet – arrived two days later. She – my daughter, and Janet too, I suppose – was young and beautiful, fashionable, intelligent.

'Hi Dad!' She said, flinging her arms around me, and I was glad of her sudden company, vibrancy, however youthful, enviable, transient it might have been. 'How have you been?'

'Good thank you,' I said, 'been keeping busy.'

'How's the telescope?'

'Oh,' I said, 'oh, it's fine. It's really good, thank you.'

'I thought you might like it,' she said.

'I do. Hello, um, Janet is it?'

'Yes,' she said, 'yes, it's Janet. Nice to meet you.' Janet held out her hand, and I shook it.

'Come on in. I'll get us a drink. Would you like red or white? Lager? Whisky?'

'Could we just have a cup of tea please Dad? It's been a long drive.'

'Of course. Yes. Sorry. Sit down.' Alice and Janet sat down on the sofa, and looked around the living room. I went through into the kitchen to put the kettle on, and when I came back Alice was standing again, looking at the photo of the Pacific from space.

'That's what distance does, eh, Dad?'

'Yes,' I laughed, not sure of the relevance, but glad of the reminiscence. 'Yes, Alice. That's what distance does. What concert are you going to see?'

'Have you heard of Dizzee Rascal?'

'No. I don't think so.'

'I've got the album here. We brought it in the car to warm us up. Do you want a listen?'

'OK,' I said. I always liked Alice's music. She put the CD into the machine and there was a moment's silence as the machine registered the CD. And then she skipped to a track.

'This is my favourite,' she said, and it started. I didn't like it. It was hip-hop. I didn't have a problem with hip-hop. I just didn't like it. This in particular was heavy, obtrusive, difficult, hacked up somehow.

'I'm not sure I like it,' I said, 'but I'm sure you'll have a good time.'

'Oh,' she said, 'we will. We're actually going to head off pretty soon, we're meeting up with some old friends from college in Leeds first.'

'OK then,' I said, 'OK. Would you like something to eat? Do you like fish?'

'That would be nice Dad. Thank you.'

Later, not long before they are due to leave, I said to Alice, 'I saw your mum the other day.'

'Yeah,' she said, 'she said.'

'Who said?'

'*She* said.'

'You didn't tell me.'

'What's to tell? She's my mum. Of course she talks to me.'

'Of course.'

I felt like I was missing something.

'I'm missing something.'

'She said that too.'

'That she was missing something?'

'That you were missing something.'

'She didn't mean it like I mean it.'

'We have to go now Dad.'

'No, Alice. We have to talk. I want to talk with you. Alice.'

'The taxi's here.'

'Don't go, Alice. I want to talk with you.' I grabbed hold of her arm. 'Alice. This is important.'

'Why?'

'Alice,' said Janet, 'we have to go.' The taxi driver started using the horn, and the sound came to me from a distance, like a foghorn, but not as loud, obviously, because it was from so far away.

Alice was leaving, looking behind her as she went, and she said, 'I'll see you later Dad, or tomorrow if you're in bed when we get back.'

'No,' I said, and she was out the door, and so far away, and the door closed, and there was silence.

★   ★

Silence. There is a photograph hanging on the wall by the stairs, and it is a photograph taken on the moon of a lunar rover in the distance. The tracks from the rover stretch all the way back to the foreground, to the camera. The sun is in the top left corner of the photograph, and glares a fierce white, and the rover tracks shine silver. Everything else is grey or black. Silence.

Utterly dead air.

I am not a silence. I am not a vampire. I am not a vacuum.

I get off the bus in Barnsley, making sure I have Siobhan's present in my pocket. Cold, hard glass. I see that the pink wash that I put down to rose-tinted bus windows is actually real. Everything is vaguely pink. Pinker, in fact, than it was before, as if the light is gradually getting redder and redder. I picture a town, a world, lit like a darkroom.
Alice gave me Siobhan's new address. It's very, very cold. I have my big coat on. I like the cold.

I reach Siobhan's house after about half an hour's walk, and I knock at the door. There is no answer. I know that this does not mean that there is nobody in; I imagine that if there is somebody in, they will not open the door. I leave the jar on the doorstep, with the thing inside, and with a note pressed against the glass.

THIS IS A FUCKING SILENCE.

The night my daughter went out to that concert, I bought a litre of whiskey and drank it all at home, with no music on, no TV, and then I took a pair of scissors from the kitchen and headed out. I didn't know where I was going until I was in the subway and I saw the graffiti. NEXT GENERATION. And I thought about my children, and I sat down against the wall, on the wet ground, wet with piss, probably, judging by the smell, and I looked at 'saddam' and I looked at 'somebody stole my spaceship', and I thought about touching the surface of the moon, I thought about not touching the Earth, and I wondered, drunkenly, if the moon would ever drift away, into the black, away from the Earth, with a backwards glance maybe, and the words that it would say if it could speak, two fingers to my orbit, fuck you all.

I thought about this planet, long dead, in a universe with no stars, and I put the scissors in my mouth, having planned this, and I pulled on my tongue, and I felt the cold metal – cold because it was a cold night – across both the top and underside of my tongue, right at the back, I had the scissors as far back as I could, and I was retching, and I slowly closed the scissors, surprised at how soft it was, how little resistance, amazed by the pain, expecting to taste the blood, but, of course, tasted nothing.

The scissors closed and I took them out of my mouth, and then closed my mouth again, my tongue still inside, dead. Entombed. After a while I put my fingers in my mouth, and tried to lick them, but there was just this feeble spasm somewhere in my throat, and I pulled my tongue out, and looked at it. Very plain for something so powerful. I threw my tongue on the floor and waited to bleed to death. Having planned this. There is a major artery in the tongue. But I didn't bleed a drop.

Out There

Paul Brownsey

– Well, terrorists have *not* blown us to bits. I'm sure it *was* a terrorist thing, Stuart. Back to normal life. Let's see who's been e-mailing us.
– Hey, Stuart, come and look at this: a whole series from someone called Beresford. A relative of my Uncle Jack? One every day we were away.
– Well, he wasn't a real uncle, just a man who lived next door when I was a boy. He was very fond of me.
– Just fond, Stuart.

> To: Rogerstamps@aol.com
> Subject: Greetings
> Date: Sat, 20 Dec 2003 18:34
>
> Dear Roger,
>   I wonder how you are getting on these days. It would be nice to hear from you.
> Very best wishes, as ever, from
> Uncle Jack

– Hey, it's actually him, Uncle Jack! He was, like, a haven in my childhood. Sometimes I'd take my homework round to Uncle Jack's and stay the night. Mum could cope better if I wasn't there. My father couldn't thump me to make her give in.
– Okay, Stuart, so I've never mentioned him before.

> To: Rogerstamps@aol.com
> Subject: Enquiry
> Date: Sun, 21 Dec 2003 18:53
>
> Dear Roger,
>   You haven't replied. There are several possible explanations for this. Perhaps you are away over the Christmas period and

have still to open my message; perhaps you have read it but opening an e-mail does not make you feel, as it makes me feel, that here is something demanding an answer *at once*, as though someone has spoken in your presence and is looking at you for your reply; or perhaps you do not want anything to do with me now.
Best wishes,
Jack Beresford

— I was, like, the son he never had. His wife died young, before they had any children, cancer. He'd take me out weekends. Taught me woodwork in his shed.

To: Rogerstamps@aol.com
　　Subject: Apology
　　Date: Mon, 22 Dec 2003 19:01

Dear Roger,
　　>perhaps you do not want anything to do with me now<
　　That could read as though I were trying to make you feel guilty about not replying. I apologise for that. Let me make it clear that you have nothing to feel guilty about, even if you choose not to reply, just as I hope I have nothing to feel guilty about.
Your
Uncle Jack

To: Rogerstamps@aol.com
　　Subject: Further apology
　　Date: Tue, 23 Dec 2003 17:16

Dear Roger,
　　>Let me make it clear that you have nothing to feel guilty about<
　　You may think, 'How arrogant the old man is, speaking like a priest who grants absolution.' Again, I apologise. That is twice I have apologised to you already, I who had hoped to have nothing to apologise for. How did we come to lose contact? My memory tells me it was merely the natural effect of your moving away after your parents' divorce, but the older one gets the less

reliable is memory.
Again, my very best wishes,
Uncle Jack

− Guilt, apologising to me, there's something a bit… But there, an old man alone at Christmas, time on his hands…
    −Yes, the divorce and moving away. I felt really guilty about not keeping in contact. But kids don't, you know, think older people can feel hurt, and as time went on… It must be, what, twenty–five years…

To: Rogerstamps@aol.com
Subject: An irrational feeling
Date: Wed, 24 Dec 2003 14:31

Dear Roger,
    Although I am trying to hold on to the idea that my e-mails lie unopened in your computer, I find that the internet gives me a strange feeling that I am in contact with you anyway, as though sending an e-mail at a precisely-registered time activates a communion of souls outside space and time, and the e-mails do not need actually to be opened and read for communication to occur. I am reminded of something I once read, that in Heaven there is no difference between one soul's intending to communicate with another and the actual achievement of communion, since without bodies there can be no obstacles between the intention and the achievement. I readily admit that this feeling, that direct communion is engendered by clicking on 'Send', is unscientific and irrational, but it is powerful for all that. Feelings that one likes to regard as irrational are often powerful. It is strange that while sending an e-mail makes me feel this, posting a letter does not. Why's that, I wonder? Do you remember that phrase? I used to say it to you. You were always a bright boy and I wanted to lead you on to exercise your mind and find out things.
Your
Uncle Jack

− *Why's that, I wonder?* − Goodness, yes, that was his phrase. It's really true:

good old Uncle Jack out there after all these years. This really is a magic Christmas present. Hey, Stuart, maybe he needs help. I owe him so much, he was the first person I told I was gay, he was so great about it. Like, a base from which I could tackle the world. I was only seventeen but he took it absolutely seriously, no you'll-grow-out-of-it stuff. 'Don't make a Faustian pact with the enemy. Hang on to your soul, because it's the only one you'll ever have.' That's what he'd say. When I asked what 'Faustian' was he made me look it up. Encouraged me to do my school project on the Faust legend. I'm sure he'd love to meet you.

> To: Rogerstamps@aol.com
> Subject: Your gift to me
> Date: Thu, 25 Dec 2003 20:24
>
> Dear Roger,
>   On Christmas night I give myself the pleasure of speaking to you yet again.

— I see what you mean: a sort of nightly treat he builds up to all day, e-mailing me.

> From my armchair I can see on the mantlepiece something you gave me for Christmas when you were ten: a little glass dome containing a scene of Victorian carollers at a house door. When shaken it releases a flurry of snow that gradually settles. To those inside the glass dome the world looks well enough, for they are exposed only to the gentle snow. No matter what giants and unspeakable monsters lie outside the dome (you and I were the monsters, Roger!), to the carollers the monsters out there do not exist and so their mouths are permanently open with carolling joy.
> Happy Christmas wherever you are, my dear Roger, from your Uncle Jack

— That ornament! I wanted to take a hammer to it to find out whether the liquid inside was just water. He wouldn't let me. He made me find out the manufacturer's address, write to them and ask.

To: Rogerstamps@aol.com
Subject: Memory
Date: Fri, 26 Dec 2003 11:06

Dear Roger,
    Physically I am in excellent shape. In the last eight years before I retired from the library I didn't have a day off because of ill-health. I still swim and cycle. Mentally, too, I think I am in excellent shape.
    I say, 'I think.'
    I have a fear that areas of my memory may have broken off and fallen beyond my reach. Do you remember the time we saw cliffs fall into the sea near Ballantrae? You talked about it for weeks. I fear I am like a farmer at the sea's edge whose fields are disappearing as the cliffs fall into the sea, section after section, and he is entirely unaware of this. The farm he still sees seems to him to be all the farm he has ever possessed.
    When I think of the man who stands behind what I do and think and say, I experience no shrinking from myself. But could it be that memories have fallen away from me that, if I recovered them, would make me feel very differently towards myself?
    My love to you still,
    Uncle Jack

– I don't like that word, Stuart, Alzheimer's. He was like a father to me, a *proper* father in place of my fucking alcoholic one.

To: Rogerstamps@aol.com
Subject: Explanation
Date: Sat, 27 Dec 2003 19:17

Dear Roger,
    Yesterday I intended to communicate something I have been preparing you for, and I funked it at the last minute. What resulted was ponderous and evasive.
    I must try to write *simply*.
    Two years ago Stanley Arne, of 146 Collingwood Road, was convicted of sexual offences against children. He had taken early retirement after a heart attack and became an unofficial child-

minder to the neighbourhood. People referred to him as Uncle
Stan. Children home from school before parents were home
went to Uncle Stan's. A mother going out for an hour would leave
her child with him. He seemed to enjoy it as something to fill up
his days. He was married, too, his wife a senior council official.
Then a girl complained about where his hands went when she
sat on his knee 'playing horses'.

– Uuuuhhhhuuuuhh...

He was convicted on three counts, involving two girls and a boy,
and got eighteen months, partly because his offences appeared
not to have gone beyond straying hands, partly because there
was medical evidence about his heart medication having
personality-changing effects. I can't remember whether he lived
in Collingwood Road when you did. His wife left him, saying she
had never suspected such tendencies. When he was due out of
prison a petition was got up against his being allowed to return
to live here. The woman who came to my door was perfectly
polite, but it was only too obvious that she was striving to keep
out of her voice and facial expression the thought, 'Here is
another old man, without even a wife: he could be up to the
same thing.' My declining to sign may have reinforced her
suspicions.

Last week I was idly looking out of the window when a police-
car came up the road, slowly, as though its occupants were
looking for a house number in this stretch. The thought came
upon me: 'This time they're coming for me.'

They weren't and the car passed on. But why did I think, 'This
time they're coming for me'? Could it be that Uncle Jack is
another Uncle Stan, but one who has conveniently forgotten
what he has done?

Everything inside my dome seems gentle and pretty but
perhaps monsters circle beyond the protective glass. You can
tell me whether they are out there. I want you to break the dome,
as you once threatened. This is one reason why I have traced
you, Roger: to put myself to the test of your memory. I hugged
you sometimes: I can feel again the texture of your fawn pullover
that unravelled at the point of the 'V' because of the way you

pulled it on and off. It was smeared with blue paint we couldn't get out, from when you dropped an Airfix model airplane you were painting. I remember the wrestling: the boys at your school had a craze for wrestling and you wanted to try out tricks on me. We did so on my bed to save your clothes from getting dirty on the floor. But in all our times together I remember nothing but what was harmless and innocent. Tell me, Roger, do you have different memories?

– I closed it because... Stuart, this is *evil*.
    – Okay, Stuart, have it your own way, he only asks *whether* something happened. There you are: open again.

Be *honest*. Honesty is the best policy: do you remember when I wouldn't let you fudge a chemistry calculation to get the right result and the teacher then said there had been a mistake in the data he'd given out?
I still dare to conclude with my love to you,
Uncle Jack

– But, see, why would he be wondering whether something happened unless he did feel like that about me when I was a boy?
– No, Stuart, I don't buy that. Feelings don't change. Like we always knew we were gay even when we were too scared to act on our feelings. If you are worried about whether you might have... done things to a boy, that means you know you *could* have done it. It means you actually *do* feel like that about children.
        – He didn't dare, that was all, living next door: Dad would have killed him and he knew it.

To: Rogerstamps@aol.com
Subject: Further explanation
Date: Sun, 28 Dec 2003 18:02

My Dear Roger,
    You will be wondering how I tracked you down. I simply typed your name into a search engine,

– See, that's what they do, tracking children through the internet, stalking them.

which led me to the web page of the Western Scottish Philatelic Association and thence to your e-mail address. The internet is a wonderful thing. And this strange sense it brings to me, of being in contact with you even if you have not yet opened my messages, is reinforced by the coincidence of the hobby to which I introduced you being the means through which I trace you.

Your look of wonder as we unfolded the first huge sheet of approvals — I recall it so vividly that my fear that important memories have fallen from me seems silly. Yet one reads of the repressed memories of abused people only coming to consciousness years later, and it stands to reason that abusers, too, may repress memories. Perhaps the police-car triggered a half-recollection that then faded out again.

Roger, tell me the truth.

My love to you,

Uncle Jack

— See, these e-mails, he's gradually building up to a confession. Like coming out as gay: first you mention it as if it had nothing to do with you personally, then you ask how people would feel if they hypothetically knew someone who was gay, and so on. That's what he's doing. He actually says in one he's been grooming me — that's what they do. Each e-mail getting closer and closer to it: *I'm a paedophile.* I bet this last one's it.

> To: Rogerstamps@aol.com
> Subject:
> Date: Mon, 29 Dec 2003 08:07
>
> Roger, please help me. Have pity. Reply.

— No, Stuart, I haven't *got* to reply.

— Because he's convinced he *did*, like, do things with me, to me, it's, like, a, what do you call it, *idée fixe*. Telling him nothing happened wouldn't serve any useful purpose.

— What are you doing? Stuart?

To: Johndberesford@btinternet.co.uk
Subject:
Date: Mon, 29 Dec 2003 21:52

Dear Uncle Jack,
   It's okay, Uncle Jack, nothing abusive ever happened.
Love,
Roger

– I won't send it, I won't. Typing a reply for me to send, it's a bloody cheek. This is *my* business.
   – Get away. Don't you dare press 'Send'. IF YOU DO, THIS RELATIONSHIP IS OVER.
   – Look, Stuart, I can't cope with this just now, my nerves are shattered enough. I really thought we were going to die. That awful shrieking clunking noise just as it's speeding up for take-off, and we're halted there a whole hour, in the dark, strapped in like the electric chair. This is it: terrorists circling out there, our plane singled out for destruction *now*. No fucking wonder he was so into hanging onto your soul, he wanted to make me an ally. That's what they do, pretending paedophiles are just an oppressed minority like gays. And when we get out, police, guns, troops, fire-engines, lights revolving: it *had* to be terrorists, whatever they said. I can't reply to him.
   – Stuart, they can trace every e-mail you send. Every website you go into. Nothing can really be wiped from a computer, it's all recorded. Not just in the computer. Out there, forever. That teacher in the paper, they knew he went into porn sites on a school computer, they tracked it, and that was grown-up heterosexual stuff. It's bad enough *receiving* e-mails like this but at least you can say it's just spam, everyone gets weird stuff. What it is, he's trying to prepare for when the police do come, trying to find out who's talked to them, find people to stand up in court and say he never abused them. But just denying someone you know is a paedophile, you'd be utterly tainted as a teacher. It'll be: *Roger Convery sends e-mails to paedophiles – no smoke without fire*. I'll be sacked. I'll be outside.
   – Outside *everything*. You're cut off, an outcast. Forever. Never safe again. Not human any more, just an outline filled with pure evil, they can do *anything* to you, like when you got labelled a witch in the

Scottish witch-craze, horrible things, rolling you down a hill in a barrel stuck with knives, you aren't *real*. How terrorists see you: just a symbol to be destroyed, not real. Christ, to think that all the time he was caring for me, putting me to bed, folding up my clothes, folding my underpants, he was... Stuart, we are so happy. We have to stay safe, safe sex is the least of it, AIDS. What's circling out there trying to get in is...

– What do you mean?

– Oh, sarcasm. 'Just carry on arranging your stamps in your albums' means I'm a horrible person who turns away from real pain to make pretty patterns with scraps of paper.

– You really don't get it, do you? This is *not* paranoia. It's all connected out there, the web, the internet, it's all beyond anyone's control, computers talk to computers, cookies, viruses… If I reply to him this address gets passed on by his computer and say he's into child porn sites and the police go into them, they'll find my address stored there, and that'll be it, they'll be breaking down OUR door. Coming for *you*, too.

– I CAN'T REPLY TO HIM. If you love me you won't make me send this.

– There goes your reply.

– Of course I haven't fucking sent it. *Deleted*, Stuart. Christ, I did delete it, didn't I? Not send? Yes. Deleted. And here go your messages, Uncle Jack; sorry, I owe you so much and it would be so easy to set your mind at rest, blah-blah-blah. *But!* Deleted, deleted, deleted, deleted. Understand, please. Please help me, Stuart. Hey, look, maybe you're right and we're communicating anyway, magic communication like souls in Heaven, so I don't *need* to reply, you're there at number 17 with my ornament on the mantelpiece, you know Roger's here with Stuart, who I love, no, whom, I remember you about *who* and *whom*. Deleted. See, they can track e-mails but they haven't got the technology to track this soul-to-soul direct communication. Yet, ha-ha. Deleted. So if we are, like, communicating, you know we're just back from New York Stamp Expo, yes, another coincidence, where Roger got a bronze medal for a display all about childhood, you gave Roger that, childhood as it's meant to be. You understand that Roger *wants* to reply. If I could just be me without all this stuff out there getting in, I'd send Stuart's message, what he wrote, but, please, it would be like putting out a message, 'This time come for *me*,' and you always wanted to protect me, you never forced Roger to reply about the bruises and things you saw that he got

from his fucking father; please, don't make him reply now, I *can't*.
– *That is disgusting, Stuart. Of course I did not fancy him.*
– Oh yes, Uncle Jack, you bet I've nothing to feel guilty about!
Deleted. Actually, these e-mails are child abuse in themselves because
they have destroyed my childhood retrospectively, *totally* fucking wasted
it. And getting home was awful because there was this terrorist scare –
okay, you didn't say you'd been grooming me, you said *prepare* – deleted
– but, Christ, same difference – and this swimming you do, so you're
hanging round swimming-pools? – advising kiddies on their strokes? –
plenty of opportunities there for *breaking down obstacles to communion* –
deleted – hey, and it wasn't just the pullover the paint got onto, did you
forget you made me take off my shirt, too? – and every second you were
aware, like, the terrorists are going to do it *now*, death – and, yes, you
admitted it, you say it, you tried to lead me on, *leading me on!* He actually
says he and I were the monsters. De–fucking–leted. All gone. And the
Trash emptied too so I can't ever be tempted to reply. Stuart, we're safe.

The Runner

Melanie Mauthner

Dusk jogger, sand runner, he pushes into the wind and sea roar. 'Lean machine,' Nadia would tease, 'all bone and muscle'.

Year in year out Istvan returns to the windswept Channel coast. Every winter he books himself an ocean room so that he can roam the shore of steel. The legacy of war surrounds him. Just beyond the beach the Atlantic Wall runs westwards around the coast. Inland, hideouts from the First World War dot the remaining forests. Every December he returns to commemorate their anniversary. On the promenade his grey shadow sways against a lamppost and for a moment, his tall frame is reflected against the river. He runs into the cream sky and touches the early moon that shimmies behind thin clouds. Istvan adjusts the marine wool hat that he wears to protect his bald head. He bought it from the family-run chandlers. But in the merciless gusts wheeling south from Siberia and the Arctic it almost flies off. He clamps it down. He bowls off again twisting through the whistling wind. He flies past hibernating sailboats. Clanking halyards knock against masts. Further along the coast city lights start to flicker. He almost detects a chugging ferry or a container ship. Soon industrial port shadows hang over the horizon. In the distance, sea spray marks the line where sea merges into sky.

He lurches onto the beach past children playing tag and onto slippery seaweed rocks. He skids on the veined ochre, then jumps onto the sand, bending his knees as he lands. By the water, seagulls cackle and gather. Far out at sea, the red lights of a freighter catch his eye. The damp seeps into his trainers and the sour seaweed smell masks his own sweat. Terns glide through the foam, skimming the low waves. Windsurfers in wetsuits careen and fly in and out of the waves slick as seals. He leaps over the puddles and they stare up at him. The wind traces ripples in the sand, leaving herringbone marks in his path.

Then he reaches the spot midway down the beach where they laid a trail of sea treasure years before. Invisible now, the cuttlefish nibs lie beneath sand smoothed by the outgoing tide. Couples walk past, scarves wrapped tight, hats pulled down, bundled snug. He hops around this shrine where they dug in tidal twine, kelp lace and fish net years ago and waited and watched for the water to reclaim them. The wind streaks the beach, sweeping its length, blowing a swathe of dust in its wake. Like a sand river it billows between the dark mud that stretches from the promenade to the wet strip at the sea's edge. Grains of salt air swirl and prickle his face and lodge in his eyes. Istvan wipes his cheeks with the cuff of his windcheater. He lengthens his strides, and with every thud, all colour in this flat light drains out of the sand.

Hazy drizzle sprinkles his thighs and as he nears the *Atlantic*, the hotel windows glow beeswax yellow. Dusk is setting in. He jogs past the seafront café and sees Nadia his fiancée with her hair pulled back in a bun. She is drinking tea and avoiding eye contact with the man opposite her – small round glasses, billy goat beard and sideburns, pensive with a cigarette in his left hand the moment before he, Istvan, proposes. He was scrawny even then before the rationing, the prisoner of war years, in the days when they first visited the resort and whiled their evenings at the Casino, later bombed out.

When he comes to the segment of coastline where fallen boulders from the eroding cliffs obstruct the way, Istvan glances up. The ruins of a bunker, decommissioned at the end of the war, perch on the cliff-top. They crumble a little more each time into the clay and chalk. He feels cold and speeds up. The wind propels him, drying out his sweat. Clouds hover illuminated from behind. As the sun sets, mussel purple hues spread in the winter sky and dissolve.

His foot dives into rotting rope and he trips. His hands plunge into the wet sand. He narrowly misses the green bottleneck pieces of glass strewn near the rope. He hoists himself up and rubs his arthritic wrist. Upright once more, he veers towards the water and notices that he is retracing his steps to the buried treasure, their hidden shrine. The tide has receded, leaving exposed his tracks from before. He circles the place where he and she pressed their collection of alabaster pen, whelk necklace and plastic brooch into the soft mud. He stops. At his feet lies a single clamshell, ivory-white: remains of their trove, he thinks.

Caressing the clam, he remembers the previous night when Nadia came to him in a dream. Hair coiled at the nape of her neck before it turned grey. Sleepwalking in their flat she shuffles barefoot. A handbag dangles from her shoulder, her nightgown soaked from another night sweat. Istvan hunts for his slim leather briefcase, arms out-stretched. He fumbles along a cool rectangular block, unsure where he left it. He tickles a calf-coloured cartable on the kitchen counter, the one he took to school as a boy. His sinewy body shakes, fingers trembling against the marble surface while he catches his breath. From across the counter, a young man peers at him over his glasses, with a thin smile. The gaunt man from the café. A second later, the springs from their bed creak and Istvan pads towards the sound from the bedroom. Nadia is lying face down, drenched and the handbag rests in the round of her back. Relieved, he shudders.

Strips of light projected through the shutter slats onto the far wall of his hotel room disorientate him. Istvan trundles over to the window, raises the electric shutter and loses himself in the full moon. He blocks out her once plump figure, long emaciated, her dishevelled white hair and crochet bed cardigan. He tries to forget her wanderings between their en-suite bathroom and master bedroom in those last months before he moved her into a nursing home. He concentrates on that tight dark bun, loose strands tucked behind her ears, hairpins sliding into her skull. His right eye twitches, his foot and wrist ache from the fall and below him, waves crash into the concrete walls of the digue. It is the high tide of the winter solstice.

The next morning, he staggers up the hill past the cemetery onto the cropped down grass. His feet bounce along the moss-soft turf, short as her salt-grey hair once it started to grow back. He curves past the bench and hurtles over the rabbit holes. He races into the playing fields trailing his hand along the nets that shelter the open land from the Channel winds. They howl through his eardrums, filling up his lungs. Lashing his face and his fingers, burning through his gloves. Another runner crosses him on the narrow path and he swears under his breath – his urge, to claim the cliff-tops for himself. Blowing in off the sea, the gusts buffet him sideways and he heads east. Soon, a pale rainbow arc mesmerises him, then disappears while hailstones pellet his oyster-catcher legs raw.

He meanders past the wild ponies grazing the grass short and plunges into the dunes. The hailstones scatter over the sand like salt crystals. When he catches one in his hand, it melts in the heat of his palm. He falls onto his knees and parts the dune grass to shelter from strong gusts. And then he stumbles upon a rabbit skull fragment. Its silky surface tails off into undulating ruffles, like the chiffon of her first ball-gown.

Long and delicate, its bone colour blends into the sand. Some of the teeth slide back and forth like a matchbox; stained dentures. Desert tones, dried up reeds, bulrushes and the scorched grass of their Moroccan honeymoon. He is sobbing now and sinks into his heels. Sea squalls brush back the icicle grass. Like the Christmas sparkle she looped into a tiara to hold back her hair. Before it fell out, before the tree stood bare and her energy seeped away. She wanted Istvan to decorate it. So she could watch him lace its branches with tinsel from the angel at the top to the parcels on their needle bed.

Frozen and vertical again, he zigzags down the slope to the bay. His feet fall heavy into the dunes like a skier in snow. He bounds over the flotsam of broken shells down to the sandpiper rocks. He fords the torrent that bites at his shins, searching out the flat dry rocks and avoids the ones buried under seaweed. After the crossing, he wipes dry his mud-splattered legs. Then a dog at his side barks at the crabs inching across the mudflats.

Suddenly, he sees her footprints, uneven steps and miniature feet. The frown she wore, afraid of what lay ahead and trying not to let it spill out. The way she pursed her lips after every mouthful and dabbed them with her napkin. The way she rolled her hands like children do in clapping games, *un, deux, trois* and looked down at them mid-sentence to see the tales they spun. The way she tilted her head to one side, looked down again slightly hunched, and then squinted up at him – 'What are you doing today? Are you going out for your run?'

Transfixed, he gazed at her and kissed her hands. Then he lowered his eyes, motioned towards the window, blinked and mumbled, 'Yes, I'll be going out soon, darling.'

After her mother died she only wore black. With her pallid skin, mollusc eyes and dyed hair, her outfits cast a mournful shadow over her delicate frame. In her coffin, Nadia lay in her winter wool dress, jet beads covering her throat. Respecting her last wish, Istvan had fished out her cashmere tights and silk undergarments. The dark stones under the water reflect back the dim December light, and the shimmer in her eyes as she laughed comes back to him. He dips his fingers into the sea stream and watches them turn purple. She died after only eighteen months of illness coursing through her bones.

Standing tall and set for the final stretch along the shore, he spots a box, washed up where the waves deposit jetsam at the high tide mark. Gulls flock to inspect it, debris from a fishing boat or a light

Channel vessel. He kicks it with his foot hard and tries to bury it but the wet sand holds it, broken and empty, with cracks down one side. Stepping back, he hears a crunch and spots the sunken hermit-crab shell. As he buries it fast before the wind scatters the particles wide, he uncovers an open razor-shell. Smaller than their clam-shell and empty. Butterfly wings, translucent as a nail, like her skin under her nightgown. The one she died in when they rushed her to hospital and he swaddled it around her shoulders in the ambulance, to keep the draught out, as she gasped and held onto his hand.

He lets the din of the sea wash over and soothe him. On the beach, he always runs where the sea carpet spreads out over the damp sand playing hide and seek with the foam. He skips when it menaces his running shoes. He surveys Goose Point at the tip of the bay and picks up a regular pace, darting in and out of the salt blasts. He soars over tidal pools. Just beyond the dulse patches where the breakers form, lie maroon waters the colour of her eyes at nightfall.

He snakes over mystery sand patterns and underground worm trails. The tide is out and flowing in. He smells waves splashing over a field of mud. At the horizon rim a darker shade of green looms. He saunters on, raw widower, sand runner. Low thunderclouds rumble and when he cranes, rain clouds lurk above the dunes. He hears it on the water before he sees it and when he looks seawards, ink stains wash the tin sky. He presses on faster, pulling his knees high up to his chest. Corrugated sand guides him along the shoreline. A blanket of rain rolls off the land and blots out the greens. Dogs and strollers scatter when raindrops speckle their coats. In an instant, the wind snuffs the passing storm and before him, the mudflats glisten.

His feet drag him back like a magnet to this coast she loved and so he returns here every year. She glides with him, flies with him kite-high, hovers above the foam where he leaves deep imprints and the water skirts and flirts with the earth. In summer, she lives just below the water. He feels her beneath the turbulence when he dives low and grazes the seabed, just as the next breaker prepares to engulf him. There he finds her underwater, in the hollow where the sea tumbles him like a ball of laundry and delivers him onto land among the bucket and sand toddlers.

Bad December

Paul Hocker

We were sitting on our bench in the pisshead's park waiting for The Champion to open at five.

'I'm sick of this,' I said, taking the beer back from Mutt. 'I came down here thinking a small town's bound to have work, but it's as fucked as the rest of the country.'

'There's worse places to be right now. What about Africa with their famine and that?'

'Mutt, I'd *rather* be in Africa than have to wake up everyday in that squat, stinking of pish, hiding from another cunt I owe money to.'

'Do you owe me money?'

I shook my head and then took a hit on the beer. The cold air had kept it chilled. The time was right to talk about escaping but I had to get Mutt interested, I needed him to come with.

'I'm off matey,' I said. 'I'm getting out of here.'

'Och, change the record, Cam. Ever since you got here you've been leaving.'

'I mean it this time. I'm giving up booze and I'm heading back to Glasgow. Me mum says she'll let me stay if I'm sober, just till I get on me feet.'

Mutt did his wheezy little laugh and stretched out on the bench. I took a last swig of beer and then threw the can onto the crazy paving. We both watched the beer froth out into a fizzing puddle. An old woman walking her dog gave a tut and skirted around the puddle. Her dog struggled to get a lick of the puddle before he was tugged away.

'We're 21 and what have we got?' I said.

'Well we did have a beer.'

'Maggie Thatcher's saying, "Here you go lads, have some money, start yourself a business," proper money if you can be bothered.'

'She also said, "Don't waste beer."'

'Think about it, we could start a gardening business or something.'

'We can do gardening here. People have gardens here. I don't want to be working for them yuppie weedgies.'

An orange Ford Capri came skidding around the corner, screeching to a halt at the park gates. Neither of us was surprised. Last Saturday night Mutt was passing the Royalty when he saw a wee blonde lass standing in the queue.

'I like a fuck and you look like you need a fuck,' he said to her. 'So why don't we fuck?'

Blondie was none too happy with this and gave Mutt a mighty boot in the bawbag and he, being wee and steaming on cider, fell on his arse and smashed his head on the kerb. He didn't come to till he got to Emergency, where I found him. 'RIP B4 XMAS' was written in Biro across his forehead, a message from Jimmy the Barn, the town psycho and cousin of the blonde in the queue who was just over from Ireland on a final visit before taking her bloody nun vows. Since then Mutt had been laying low.

But not low enough. Jimmy's big red face burst out of the orange Capri's sunroof.

'Mutt, ye cunty-fuck.'

By the time Jimmy clambered out of his car and into the pisshead's park we were pegging it through the shopping arcade and onto Castlehead estate. Mutt's nan lived in flats on the estate and he knew where the spare key was so we ducked in there.

We sat in the dark in front of the electric fire and caught our breath.

'I'm off tonight, Mutt.'

'To Glasgow?'

'No, I'm gonna get sober first. I don't want to get to Glasgow wanting a drink.'

'Where you gonna do that then?'

'I'm going up Eskdalemuir till the New Year.'

'Up the Eskie? Oh fuck, that's a cold fucking Christmas, so it is.'

'You'll have a cold Christmas when Jimmy finds you, lying out in the morgue.'

'Och, that bag of guts can get tae fuck. I've been running from him since nursery school.'

There was dust on one of the electric fire's orange bars and it crackled and hissed.

'Mutt, let's quit the booze together. You've said yourself that the booze was gonna kill you, like it killed your old man. My old man's locked up in Berlinnie cos of booze. It's booze that broke your nose. It's always fucking booze, Mutt, and it doesn't fucking change cos we're too pished-up to change it.'

'Something's always gonna get you, Cam. A bus could knock you down tomorrow.'

'Aye, and there's no buses up the Eskie, so that's okay.'

'I'm not sleeping rough in nae forest.'

'Right enough, cos neither am I.'

'Eh?'

It was time to play my trump card.

'There's a foxhole, a secret den. We built it when I was in the scouts. It's a proper bunker with a tin roof and planks and a ladder.'

I could almost see the cogs in Mutt's tiny head begin to turn.

'We'll go native, Mutt, live off the land. I can keep a fire going while you go out hunting and meanwhile, without really doing anything, we'll kick the booze.'

I knew Mutt would like the survival part of the plan. He loved all the Rambo films.

'So you'll need weapons, crossbows and spears and that,' Mutt said, trying not to sound too interested. 'They're not so hard to make if you know what you're doing. You just need a good knife and some wire.'

I was about to tell him about all the traps and snares we could set when a brick came through the window, showering glass on Mutt's head. I looked out to see Jimmy the Barn leaning out of his orange Ford Capri.

'Yees are deed. Think my wee cousin's a whore? Eh Mutt? Eh? You minky basturt. I'm gonna tango on your puss, yee sleekit wee basturt.'

Mutt shook the glass out of his hair.

'Eskie eh? I think me nan's got a sleeping bag I can borrow.'

Mutt was trying to kill a blackface sheep. He was trying to cut its throat with his kiddie penknife but the sheep was not having it, so he had to sprawl across the beast to keep it still.

'Oh fuck man, you could at least buy her a drink.'

'Get to fuck, Cam, this is dinner, pal.'

Mutt was trying to find its neck under the thick wool.

'Give it here, man.'

'Leave off, Cam, I'm nearly done.'

'You're nearly nothing. Give me the knife, Mutty.'

Mutt began slicing the knife back and forth across the sheep's thick neck.

'I'm doing it.'

'You're doing shite, Mutt. You look like you're playing the violin. Give it here.'

Mutt pulled the knife away and then fell back, almost catching his shoulder in the fire.

'Fuck. Fucking thing.'

'What have you done man?'

'I've stabbed meself.'

Mutt gripped his thigh and swore at the sheep, calling it a 'woolly whore.' The sheep got to its feet, shook itself and then trotted back into the forest.

'Stop whining, man, let's have a look at it.'

It was very minor, a wee nick, but I wrapped my towel tightly around his leg to keep him quiet.

'Is that clean? I don't want an infected leg.'

'Are you cummin' the cunt, Mutt? That's my towel you're bleeding all over, by the way.'

'Shit, Cam, I hate blood. Bloody sheep. How do I stop bleeding?'

'Just press on the towel, you'll be fine. I won't be long.'

'What? Where are you going? You said we were staying here until the New Year.'

'We are but we need plasters and stuff.'

'We don't need plasters, this towel's fine. Plasters are for bairns anyhow.'

I rolled him a fat joint and as soon as he got puffing he wasn't bothered by the leg or me leaving. It was nearly dark, getting on for five and I reckoned I could get back down to the road and into town in time for the chemist.

'Watch out for Jimmy the Barn? He'll give ye a beatin' if he sees you, and then he'll come up here and kick the cunt out of me.'

'He won't see me. Jimmy works late in the butchers. They'll be cleaning out the back room till gone seven.'

'Be quick then, man, I get bored on me own.'

'Aye, I'll do my best.'

'Cam, do us a favour. Get us a porno while you're there.'

The beech trees were bunched close together and even with my torch I couldn't see much but black so I had to rely on my ears. I held my breath and listened for the road until I heard its faint whooshing sound, like waves on a beach. I headed toward the sound, stopping every now and again to make sure I hadn't drifted. As the road got louder I was able to move quicker with my head down, smashing through the branches until the trees started to thin out. I got a lift from a Christian hippy in a campervan and within minutes the familiar orange glow of Lockerbie's streetlights appeared.

A Geordie businessman in a BMW picked me up on the way back. He was playing the Pet Shop Boys and I knew straight off he was a buftie so I kept my arse tight on the passenger seat. But he was a gentleman because when I told him I was spending New Year up in the forest he gave me a full packet of fags and a wrap of coke to see in Hogmanay. A whole fucking gram of cha-cha bingo! I'd have let him touch my arse for half as much.

On the walk back from the road to the forest the coke began burning a hole in my pocket and I couldn't resist a wee taste. I sat down cross-legged in the well of a steep furrow, stuck the wrap in the chemist's bag and opened it up. The wind was fierce so I put my face in the chemist's bag and woofed up a nostril full of coke. I snorted it back and felt the acid taste at the back of my throat. Soon enough I was on a decent rush, flopped back on the soil and riding the wave.

'Who'd want the booze with this gear, eh? This is me in Glasgow son, this is you with a nice car, nice house. Get yourself an executive box at Rangers, all me pals and a page-three blondie on me knobbie. This is me, lad. Fuck yes, no doubt there.'

I thought about taking a second wee chaser when a ball of light appeared above me. It was a silent fiery rip in the sky that kept getting bigger. I thought I was tripping out and that I was seeing a floating red carnation. Then there was a furious sound about twenty-seconds later; God bringing up a greenie, two meteors slamming together, a penny-piece dragged over a chalked board. It was all these things and it echoed around the hills like a ghost. I wasn't tripping; I was watching a jet plane coming to pieces.

At the centre of the flaming ball were small black shapes swirling around three larger sections that were falling quickly.

One of the pieces looked like it was heading directly for Lockerbie. It was a wing and it was on fire and after a long, twisty fall, the wing disappeared between the hills and moments later the ground shook. My first thought was of the girl in the chemist I'd flirted with not twenty minutes ago. Then I thought of the boys drinking in The Champion. I even thought of Jimmy the Barn.

The sky was now full of falling pieces and some of them were burning. It was hard to tell which direction they were coming so I ran toward the edge of the forest for cover just as a pair of seats landed hard in the soil twenty yards ahead of me, stopping dead. Then another pair of seats crashed down to my right, tumbling a few times over the ground before settling upright. A man and a woman, still holding hands, were strapped into their seats. Their bodies were all wrong. Arms, legs, heads, all twisted about. I knew they were dead but I couldn't help but shout over to see if they were alright.

Stuff was coming down in the trees in front of me, branches were snapping and thick smoke was building up. It smelt of burnt rubber. I got under one of the larger trees on the edge of the forest and watched the stuff fall out of the sky. I heard a movement above me, like a creaking, and I looked up and thought I saw someone. I shone my torch into the branches and lit up the dead eyes of a wee lad in a tracksuit, his arms outstretched like he was reaching out for help.

I went and sat on the open land and smoked for Scotland as the emergency sirens came closer. I sat there, crying for the first time in years, staring straight ahead at the flames coming up out of Lockerbie, thinking about the girl from the chemist and the lad in the tree. Then I heard something rattling behind me. I swung about to see a figure in the smoke. It was limping. It was Mutt.

'Mutt?'

'Whey-hey!'

Out of the smoke he came, pushing the plane's battered drinks trolley. He had tied a red bandana around his head Rambo style.

'Fuck the drying out, Cam. God wants us pissed.'

He kicked the sliding side panel on the trolley open and helped himself to two wee plastic whiskey bottles. He threw one over to me and I held it in my shaky hands, squeezing the bottle tightly. The sirens were getting louder.

'This is not the way, Mutt. A drink is not going to make this never happen.'

When I looked up again Mutt was gone.

The police, ambulances and fire crews were the first to arrive. Then the TV people parked up on the A47 and set up their dishes. Finally men in white plastic suits appeared, bringing with them huge lights and petrol generators. The police unrolled a tape barrier while the men in plastic measured where the people had landed. All this work went on around me.

A detective, a lady, asked me if I was okay and what I was doing there.

'I don't know, Luv, I really don't know.'

She put a blanket on my shoulders and then answered her radio. She was being called back to Lockerbie. 'It's a mess, the Shell station exploded,' said the voice on her radio.

'Are you going to be okay? There's people arriving soon you can talk to,' said the detective.

'Don't worry about me, I'll be fine. You get on.'

The detective was called away and shown a battered Christmas present lodged in the ground. It had snowmen on the wrapping paper. The detective ordered a cordon around the gift and radioed for a bomb disposal unit.

I slipped away out of the light, away from the people and back toward the foxhole. The last person I saw that night was a fireman taking a piss in the trees.

'Alright mate?' he said. 'Are you looking for someone?'

He zipped up his flies and buttoned up his thick yellow jacket.

'No, it's okay,' I said, throwing him the whiskey bottle. 'I think I know where he is.'

Perfect Day

Suzanne Batty

What a perfect day on which to drown.

I push myself out into the water, past the flowering water lilies, their long green ropes disappearing into the depths. I carry my disappointment like a weight in my stomach, but it is not heavy enough and my swimming costume has no pockets for stones. I am thinking about Dr Nolan. It's hard to take advice from someone with a voice like bone. What a perfect day to take your medication, exercise gently, read (but not too much), keep to a routine.

This is my routine. I breathe in as I bend my arms and legs and out as I stretch, and in this way I move across the lake like a waterboatman and I keep my head from setting on fire.

It is safe in the water. Safe from hospitals and relatives and people on stations who stare.

All around the edge of the lake people are eating cold chicken and ham sandwiches and shouting at their children. A dog crashes into the water and I can see his wet otter head swimming towards me.

In the dayroom they will be smoking and bickering and the small black woman who never sits still will be walking up and down, turning the music up and the paranoid man will be talking to granddad about fishing and the thin girl will be running for the door. They will all be there on this perfect day with the curtains closed and the windows locked. I would be there too, except that I am in the lake, swimming.

On the bank is a small blue bag which now belongs to me. The shop was cool and lovely and full of useful things. I chose the blue bag, a jumper, a sleeping bag, my turquoise swimming costume and a tiny stove you could fit in your pocket and the woman said are you going somewhere nice and I said I don't know I'm just going.

I walked through the town and into the woods by the river. There were people by the river and the woods were full of chip papers and beer cans but after a while there were less people and then no people and I was alone. I wasn't thinking anything. I listened to the lonely birds in the pines and to my feet moving and I knew if I could walk I would feel better, if I could get to the lake I would be well.

But when I get to the lake I know I will never be well.

I remember the collapsing woman and the nurses shouting get up Julia get to your room and that's when I stood up and walked past the office and nobody saw me. I opened the door and I kept on walking.

But what will I do now, now that I am swimming in the lake? What will Dr Nolan be saying in his bony voice when they discover me gone? I will end the story. I will end it like this. I will look at the trees leaning over the lake and the distant mountains. I will look at the sun and the perfect blue sky. Then I will take a deep breath and dive into the water, down to where it is cold and dark, past the water lilies' long green ropes, far away from the waterboatmen. The perfect day will be no more. The perfect day will have ended.

Marginalia

Crista Ermiya

Today, in the reading room, you examine a facsimile of a thirteenth-century bestiary, carefully separating each page with your gloved fingers. The original codex comes from a monastery in the North of England. You imagine the naked fingers of damp monks freezing tight around their quills, the chafing of chilblained hands as they create a universe of sun-darkened, heat-hardened mammals, exuberantly scaled reptiles, tropical plants with phalluses for flowers, or unipods – one-legged almost humans – who hop along on one enormous foot, and use it as a canopy against the scorched daylight of an eastern desert.

You love this book. It is your favourite in all the world. In this book the margins at last come to the centre. Monsters and marvels rub along together, verso to recto. In this book the freaks have top billing, while the margins are populated with the mundane: plain monks in ordinary brown cowls, scribing, praying, farming; or drinking ale and coursing, hares and foxes making good their escape in the foliated corners of the page.

And what difference between a monster and a marvel, you want to know as you turn the pages beneath your gloves. You have examined this book many times. You ponder the nature of monstrosity daily.

The book falls open at a picture of a unicorn, its horny head lain down upon the thighs of a virgin. You think, *I have never been kissed.* You touch your lips under the net veil of your hat, but cannot feel them through your gloves.

You first notice him on Monday. He sits next to you at the catalogue terminal, and you watch him fill out the search with book titles you cannot quite read from here. He glances up sideways at you and smiles. You want to smile back. Your hands go up to your hat, adjust your veil slightly, pull it further down in front of your face. You undo the button of your high-neck blouse, then re-button it. You fumble, but not because of the gloves. You are used to doing everything wearing gloves. You watch him get up and take a seat at a desk. You leave the catalogue terminal to sit down at your own seat: you can watch him from here.

You observe how his dark wavy hair falls in front of his eyes while his head is bowed towards the reading material in front of him, so that he has to brush it back with his hands, again and again. You can feel the slick of his hair oil sliding onto his hands, as if they were your own hands and you had no gloves, instead leaving a trail of dirty fingerprints on the filmy paper of your books. You wonder if he noticed where you sat down. You are afraid he will look up and see you. You are afraid he won't look up.

On Tuesday there is an unfamiliar woman behind the desk. The others are used to you by now, but she stares as you queue to collect your books. You hear her ask another member of staff whether readers are allowed to keep hats and gloves on in the reading room. The librarian follows her gaze, realises she is referring to you, and gives her a lengthy reply that you do not hear. She nods and continues fetching the called-up books. You hope that someone else will serve you, but when you get to the head of the queue she is the one who asks for your desk number. When she speaks, it is clear that the other librarian has explained your situation to her, your special dispensation. She tries to sound casual and friendly, but doesn't. You look at her mouse-coloured hair, her thin taupe lips, her timid forehead. She is plain and mundane like the monks in the margins of your beloved manuscript.

You think, *no-one would notice her if she walked into a room*. You tell her your desk number and she gives you your books. When you turn around, the dark-haired man you met at the catalogue terminal yesterday is behind you. You blush, you feel as red as your suit, and almost drop your books. But he has already stepped up to the counter. You walk back to your desk.

You don't normally take a break for lunch, but at noon on Wednesday when you see the dark-haired man get up and put on his jacket, you decide to get up too and follow him outside. At the door you have to show your clear plastic bag to the security guard so that she can examine the contents inside. Then you are free to walk out into the public area, where you follow him into the self-service canteen. You watch him pick up a tray from a pile, so you do the same.

'Hello,' he says.

'Hello,' you reply, but it comes out as a croak, because the only other words you have spoken, all week, were to tell the library staff your desk number, and to ask for a travelcard at the newsagents. You clear your throat and pretend you are recovering from a cold.

'Great hat,' he tells you. 'I love all those old black and white movies.'

What luck. He imagines that's why you dress like this, why you wear a hat with a net veil, the gloves that always conceal your hands. You wonder if he might think you affected, as people often do.

'Michael,' he says, holding out his hand. You hold out your gloved hand in return. You cannot feel the texture of his fingers or his palm – only their slight pressure on yours – but when you shake hands a shock of static runs between you. You pull back quickly with an embarrassed croak and pick up your tray again. You tell him your name.

'That's a pretty name,' he says. 'Where's it from?'

It's always your name that gives you away, underneath the hat and the gloves and the clothes, underneath the voice that sounds just like theirs. You tell him its origin and he nods. You notice that his eyes are grey in the light of the canteen. In the reading room they had appeared a dark shade of blue. In either case, they stir you to breathlessness: like the start of a panic attack. You sit down together for lunch, although you only have a cold drink on your tray, in a carton with a straw.

'I don't normally have lunch,' you explain.

You raise the straw to your lips, underneath the netting. You know that lunch is a bad idea because he can see that you won't take your hat off, nor your gloves, not even to eat or drink. You watch his face as he realises for the first time that he cannot see any part of you beneath your clothing. He focuses instead on the tray in front of him, on the sandwiches he has chosen, his apple and pot of tea.

He asks about your research and you tell him about the manuscripts, about the margins with their monsters and beasts, and all the fell creatures that have no place other than on the edges of things.

'Monsters?' He smiles. 'Like those maps that say 'Here be dragons'?'

His own research is on British naval history. You tell him about the maps where the world is a circle divided by a seascape in the form of a cross, with its top limb missing. You explain about the earthly paradise, in the east; you explain that the closer to paradise, the more densely populated with monsters.

'Britain,' you tell him 'appears on such maps as a strange cold island in the far west, as far away from paradise as can be imagined; a little thing populated by ghosts, right on the edge of the world.'

This makes him smile too, but as you would to the frayed old man who sits next to you on the bus and sings, unravelling his lunatic tunes from stop to stop.

When you get home that night you don't immediately take off your hat and gloves but you do unbutton your coat. You feel hot. It's not just the contrast with the cold night outside. You can feel the heat rising through your body, underneath your clothes, underneath your hair and skin. You peer into the dim mirror in the bathroom, the only mirror in your flat, and hold your gloved hands up to the sides of your face beneath the netting of the Forties-style hat. Only shadows can be seen beneath the veil, the fact that you have eyes and a mouth. You turn, first one way, then the other. Beneath the stylized clothing you look normal. *This is all he sees*, you say to yourself. And then you call his name out loud into the flat: *Michael*. But the empty echo makes you shiver, despite the flush you can feel working its way up your spine. You cover over the mirror with a towel and undress with your eyes closed.

On Thursday you make notes on a facsimile of a fourteenth-century travelogue. On one leaf is a line drawing, with a scrolled caption at the bottom that reads, when translated into English, as 'Community of Monsters'. Once there existed an accompanying text that revealed the nature of their monstrosity but that page is now missing – torn out or burnt. You examine the surviving picture closely, as you always do, trying to work out why these particular creatures were deemed monstrous. They look human to you, these half-dozen naked men and women living in caves in a desert oasis, hunting, cooking. Gentle brushstrokes across their skin indicate hair, a bristly down that covers their entire bodies. Are they monsters because of their wild-pig hairiness? Or because they refuse to cover it up? You imagine them dressed in the clothes of the people around you in the reading room, and as you look around you see Michael sitting in a far corner, head bent low, hands brushing away the curling hair from his forehead. You've never seen him sit so far back before. You wonder if he is avoiding you.

On Friday he fails to see you behind him in the queue for the counter. The new librarian is serving again.

'Good morning Susan,' you hear him say.

'Hello Mike,' she replies. *Mike?*

Susan goes to fetch his books. She takes her time handing them over. You notice that their fingers touch. She sees you in the queue and blushes. Michael turns in the direction of her blush. You watch him take in your costume. He nods a half-smiled good morning to you, glances back to Susan, and takes his books.

Susan puts on her false, bright smile and asks for your desk number, slowly and loudly as if you might have difficulty understanding. You don't answer at first, just stand there staring at her. Her hair is the colour of dishwater after you have spilled cold coffee in the sink. Her eyes are the colour of unwashed beer bottles held up to the light. Her lips are thin as the tapered ends of chopsticks. You want to slap her in the face, hard. You want to set a stopwatch on how long it would take the bright red mark of your gloveprint to fade. Instead you give her your desk number. She gives you your books.

But she is nervous; her gaze has faltered under your gaze and her hands grow sweaty. The books fall. You look down at them, see where they have fallen to your feet, see your shoes that are so thick with shine and polish that you could, if you wished, lift your veil and look at your distorted image in their curved reflection.

'I'm so sorry,' Susan wails.

You don't say anything, but bend to retrieve the disarrayed volumes. And somehow you become unbalanced as you bend down. You tumble sideways. You become disheveled. A reader behind you – you don't know whether it's a man or a woman – reaches out a hand to steady you, but you push them away. Susan gasps. You quickly adjust your hat, your veil, but it's too late. She has already seen your face.

'Oh my god,' she says.

'Sssshhh,' hushes one of the other librarians, mortified at Susan's lapse of tact. Still, Susan stares at your veiled hat in horror, at your gloves, at your high-button blouse. Other staff and readers gather at both sides of the counter and pretend not to peer at you.

'But there's nothing wrong with her,' says Susan.

You think, *she sounds genuinely disturbed.*

'There's nothing wrong with her.'

'What?' asks Susan's colleague. And like her, he has only enough words to repeat himself: 'What?'

You sense them watching you as you straighten up with the books, walk back to your desk and quietly get on with your research. Whenever you look up, in whatever direction, heads slide away, as if they had been turned to you only a moment before. Only later do you remember Michael. You look up from your books. You look up, but you cannot see him anywhere.

You turn the pages of your favourite bestiary, and trace a gloved index finger around the monstrous outlines centre-paged, marveling at the variety of deformity. Your finger follows the curve of the Blemeye, a headless creature that wears its face on its torso. The Blemeye holds up a club and brandishes it at a Cyclops. In turn the one-eyed giant holds in its expansive hand a squint-eyed Pygmy wielding a bow and arrow. Blemeye, Cyclops and Pygmy stare out at you from the manuscript. Below these creatures, the unknown scribe has inked-in the figure of a girl, ordinary and plain, squeezed tight into the margin. She sits with her face half-hidden as she reads a tiny book, right off the edge of the text.

Peter and Elsie

Andy Murray

Jamie had never been to a funfair, being a retiring, sheltered sort of lad, but when one came to the park by the campus, Louise dragged him along. In the winter dusk, he threaded his lanky frame amongst the crowds to stay by her side, muddy rainwater soaking into his turn-ups. At first the scene was quite dazzling, as though entirely composed of smoke, neon and blaring sirens, and Jamie's beleaguered senses were almost swamped. He imagined the Blitz must have been pretty similar, only without the degree of free will. Big Wheels loomed and waltzers wailed around them, spitting out dance hits like tinny thunder, and Jamie shook his head wonderingly at the thought of sane folk enjoying such treatment.

Louise could handle a bit of noise but she could take or leave the rides, so they simply explored hand in hand. At first it was an experience they observed, rather than engaged with, scoffing candy-floss and watching their breath make steam in the air. Once they'd acclimatised, even Jamie found himself quietly enjoying the odd panoply of smells and sounds and lights. They each had a fruitless turn on the fruit machines, which nevertheless generated a faint thrill. Then they fed a steady trickle of copper change into a grinding coin waterfall. For a time they stood watching parents watching their children glide on a bright, chiming merry-go-round. Feeling less intimidated, they found a stall where they tried throwing hoops over plastic frogs in a pretend pond, but they were too busy watching each other and sniggering to concentrate properly on their aim.

With their last pooled pound coins in hand, they wandered over to the rifle range. Bereft of punters, the long-faced stall-holder was sitting perched on the counter, reading the sports pages. Quite out of the blue, Louise's face lit up, and seconds later she was squinting through the sights. She proved to be a dab hand. Jamie stood and watched with a dash of alarm as she put three dead-eyed holes in a piece of card with a target symbol. As a prize, from a harshly lit wooden shelf, the stall-holder handed them a dinky cuddly rabbit, short-haired and light brown, with a curiously stern expression. It was somehow indisputably, instantly a 'she'. So she promptly travelled home in Louise's roomy parka pocket, her nose and ears poking out into the night air, with Louise keeping a cradling hand on her at all times. For a day or two they batted names about, before they decided to call her Elsie. Almost unbidden, the rabbit began to sleep in their bed, tucked between the pillows.

Jamie had never really had a proper relationship before he met Louise. He'd had girlfriends back home, but those experiences had all been fleeting and altogether a bit pointless. This was serious. Except, that was just it: it wasn't serious at all. He and Louise spent entire days making one another laugh. They could tell each other anything, whatever mood they were in, or secrets that they had. It seemed almost too easy.

They'd met in a bustling queue at the university cafeteria in the second week of term, and Louise had managed to draw him into conversation. She was smiley and petite, sporting vivid, reclaimed Seventies clothes and a jet-black pageboy bob. They went on to spend a coy, exciting afternoon, and thereafter a revelatory night, together. That was it. Within a month they were, to all intents and purposes, sharing a room.

Jamie relished the long days spent roaming charity shops and fetching bulging bags of food from the supermarket. As a boy he'd been a solitary soul, never happier than when sat with his nose in a book, or playing his records on a little hand-me-down stereo. Louise, on the other hand, was more worldly. She'd had a rough-and-tumble childhood and knew her way around a boy, yet the two of them had meshed perfectly. In private, which was, after all, the lion's share of the time, the L-word was used freely between them, and they called each other secret pet names. They were inseparable, and both as surprised about it as the other.

After they'd been together just over a year, the pair of them moved to a dilapidated first-floor flat on the outskirts on the city, living above a slightly scary old lady who stunk of antiseptic. Somehow, though, life had changed, and by agonising, silent degrees, things between them began to get a little fractious. At first they relished spending days on end in each other's company, but now they were secretly feelingly guilty at the pleasure they took in being apart, however briefly: working, or walking to the shops, or doing the washing-up.

That was when Peter and Elsie came along.

Louise's fruitful sharpshooting at the fair became the start of a cuddly toy obsession, or something very close. On summer day-trips to Blackpool they'd parade slowly down the Golden Mile, spending endless bags of 10ps in the arcades, and invariably they'd have a new addition or two to take home on the train. All these animals lived on the bottom of their double bed, at least at first. Within a year, there were too many of them to fit on, but they always had a special soft spot for little Elsie.

Much to his own surprise, Jamie discovered he relished playing the arcade crane machines. He knew they were a fix, and that they didn't grab sufficiently on every go, but that meant it wasn't entirely a game of skill, of which he was convinced he had none anyway. Instead, luck was involved, which made it quite exciting. There was never any question of Jamie trying for digital watches or cheap jewellery. He went for the cuddly toys every time.

On one long afternoon, Jamie poured coin after coin into such a machine, having taken a shine to the furry creatures within. His perseverance eventually paid off when the metal claws deposited a tiny cuddly dog down the chute. He was wearing bright blue spotted dungarees, with a red felt tongue, sitting up excitedly. Jamie christened him Peter.

The strangest thing happened when Peter was taken home and met Elsie. She suddenly came to life – insofar as Louise picked the rabbit up and moved her about. Elsie began whispering into Louise's ear, Sooty fashion, and developed a character. Now Elsie was naughty and devious, and she'd do anything in the pursuit of her real love, chocolate. Louise had Elsie pretend nibbling from her Dairy Milk. She also liked to dance about.

Peter was her other half, her oppo. Peter was sweet and innocent, and, under Jamie's supervision, he was wont to sway excitedly, making his floppy black ears flap madly. Peter was also Elsie's conscience, and would chide her when she was selfish or rude. He communicated in a series of yaps that only Jamie, Louise and Elsie could translate. He was very fond of singing and cuddling up. Together the surly-looking rabbit and over-enthusiastic dog were a perfect, if unlikely match: a three-dimensional cartoon, part Walt Disney, part Road Runner.

In no time at all there was a new hierarchy amongst the cuddly toy community. Peter and Elsie were quietly crowned king and queen, the favourites, the ones who always made it into the bed at night, even when space was tight. The others – an elephant, a seal, a monkey, all named and the list went on – became defined by their relationships to the main two. Their leaders were always friendly and kind, but they'd invariably be the stars of amassed adventures. A later addition, a minuscule teddy bear, actually became Peter's own cuddly toy. Peter even got Elsie Christmas presents.

Wherever Jamie and Louise went, Peter and Elsie would follow. They came back home with them during the term holidays, always packed safely near the top of a bag. Sometimes they'd sneak unseen into lectures too, hiding in a carrier. Whenever Louise got into a foul mood and stormed off, there would always be a little 'arf!' at the door half an hour later, and Peter would peek round to break the ice. (When Louise's beloved Gran died, Peter and Elsie were respectfully quiet for a week or two, but eventually it was their mischief that cheered her up again.)

Elsie would habitually be found hiding in cupboards by packets of confectionery, or Peter would be waiting outside the bathroom door when someone got out of the shower. They'd get excited about birthdays and favourite chart acts. In truth, Jamie and Louise's relationship gradually became more like that of playmates than of lovers, but they both adored curling up on the bed with the little dog and tiny, naughty rabbit. It wasn't really something they could share with other people. They didn't exactly think there was anything wrong with it, but nor did they feel they could discuss it in company.

But then, they never went out much anyway.

There were times when they found it hard to drop the Peter and Elsie noises and just talk normally. Occasionally, Louise would find herself holding Peter for a change, conversing with Jamie 'being' Elsie. They'd share an awkward glance: it was hard to express, but somehow that wasn't right at all.

Once they graduated, Louise got a well paid PA job in a successful city centre office, and she began to harbour secret feelings for a guy who worked there, if not two. Jamie sort of knew. By the end of that year, he was working part-time in a bookshop squirreled away off the high street, and had taken a fancy to a sparkly-eyed female colleague himself. The pair of them had put on a bit of weight: good living, they'd call it, sheepishly. But neither was the same vibrant young thing the other had fallen for. Physically, things between them had gone awfully quiet. With increasing frequency, they'd go out drinking separately with their own friends, or else long-estranged mates from back home would visit for bonding weekends. The two of them became disparaging about one another's taste in music and films, whereas once they'd gone to great pains to be impressively open-minded.

They stuck together, but in dark moments alone, it would strike them that the perfect relationship they'd happened across in the cafeteria that day was beginning to look dog-eared. Louise was pretty ambitious and was doing well for herself. Jamie wasn't all that bothered about such things, but noticed she didn't make an effort with her dress sense like she used to. (These days it was all trouser suits and shoes with sensible heels.) Louise would often return home to find the flat in a state and fire off a shot across Jamie's bows. She'd spend weary evenings watching brain-off telly, while he sat up reading in the kitchen 'til the wee small hours.

In passing they'd discuss commitment: getting married, getting a house, even maybe having a baby, but only in a cursory, half-hearted fashion, as though they simply thought they should talk that way after being together so long. Similarly, the L-word would still be tactically deployed, but increasingly with a frown, and a lack of eye contact. They were both far happier getting their shoes off on the double bed and playing with Peter and Elsie, sniffing out chocolate, hiding and dancing.

Late one Saturday afternoon, as autumn beckoned, they were walking though the local precinct, rowing furiously. Louise had started lending Jamie money, and keeping a close record of what he owed. She was dipping heavily into her building society account, and there was no sign of Jamie being able to start repaying the debt. Indeed, the total kept on escalating. Jamie had just asked sheepishly for another tenner to buy a CD, and Louise had gone mental. It was only a little thing, but as the bruising recriminations were slung back and forth, neither could summon up the energy to back down and make up. It began to feel like a falling-out on a different scale entirely. Louise wouldn't let Jamie touch her, and openly snarled at him in the queue in the newsagent's.

By the time they arrived at Barnardos, they hadn't spoken a word in half an hour. They detached off to their own favourite corners of the shop – Louise, clothes and fabrics; Jamie, the second-hand books – and tried to pretend they were focused on browsing. When Jamie could bear the atmosphere no longer, he went over to find Louise motionless before the children's toys. He knew immediately that something was wrong. She was staring numbly at a white wire rack filled with unwanted toys. There, perched at the top, was a cuddly beige dog, tongue lolling. Its dungarees were lime-green. It was a bright lime-green Peter.

Jamie put a comforting arm round Louise's shoulder, and shook her gently out of her daze. Suddenly Louise grabbed Jamie and cuddled him, almost painfully hard. Gasping back sobs, she pleaded loudly into his ear, 'What's going to happen?'

'Who's going to look after them when we're gone?'

By Christmas, they'd gone their separate ways. It was an enormous upheaval, but in the event it felt entirely natural: something of a relief, even. It had long since dawned on them that they weren't going to stay together forever after all. Jamie got custody of the cuddly toys. They'd tried to laugh about it. After a fractious few months, they barely kept in touch at all.

But Jamie could never give Peter and Elsie away, and he made sure to keep them, if admittedly right out of the sight of girlfriends, at the very least somewhere nice and dry and safe.

The Rats

Graham English

We're making love when Evie hears a noise. I say making love, but it's fucking.

'Scurrying,' she says, 'in the attic.'

Evie has amazing ears. Amazing to look at with their tiny, soft lobes, but more so in the way they work: like a sleeping dog's or cat's for noises; like a part-time deaf person's for conversation or calling through the house. She's never seen a doctor about it. Fair enough, it's something you learn to live with. She puts it down to her dad but he doesn't have the sleeping dog-cat thing and lip-reads on the odd occasion he wishes to communicate.

'That's it again, but louder. Can't you hear it?'

She climbs off of me.

'It's got to be mice, or rats. Oh my God, rats Tommy.'

She switches her bedside light on, gets out of her side of the bed and puts on her robe. She looks up at the attic hatch and then over at me.

'Will you go up?'

'I'll go up in the morning,' I say.

'Won't you go up now?'

'No.'

'What if they're gone in the morning?'

'Then end of problem.'

'I can't hear them now either. They'll have gone quiet because they've heard us talking.'

'Maybe they're trying to make out the words.'

Evie doesn't say anything.

'Evie?'

'What?'

'I'll go up in the morning. If there's any sign, I'll put something down or call pest control.'

117

'Do you promise?'

'Promise.'

'They're going to keep me awake. As soon as we're quiet they'll start up again.'

'Then let's make some noise and fall into a deep, dark sleep.'

She takes a last look up at the hatch, lets her robe fall open, switches off the light and climbs back in to the bed.

'Quickie,' she says. 'I want that sleep and I need to get away early in the morning. You'll have to do the kids yourself.'

'Fine,' I say.

After a long drought we've been having sex again, urgently, and often. I don't know why and Evie being Evie I know that if I say much about it the spell will break. Probably she has given herself permission to fantasise again or there is somebody new she is trying not to sleep with; probably both. I am who I am and I am never going to turn it down with Evie. Especially now. Because after nine years together, six of them married, I'm at last holding *Evie*; now that we fuck with the lights off and we're not kissing. We have finally become experts in each other's bodies who can fuck to fit Evie's schedule. Occasionally we have a full take-your-time meeting but usually we have any-other-business moments, in what Evie, being a half traditional, half modern woman, calls *a quickie*.

Maybe I am a half modern, half traditional man: modern in that it is my job to look after Danny and Rachel, our children; traditional in that I agreed to slaughter our potential rats. Evie, who works long hours as a lawyer by day, and for that matter by night, reaffirms the rats part of our contract as she leaves the house. Danny, Rachel and I are talking over toast when she calls through from the front door.

'Tommy, do not forget to tackle the situation forthwith. I remind you that you have promised. See you all later.'

We call back a goodbye but it only finds Evie's ears and then a closing door.

'What situation?' asks Rachel.

'We might have mice, or maybe even big fat rats, hunting for munchies in the loft.'

'Cool,' says Daniel.

'Not cool. Disgusting,' says Rachel.

'Fact of life,' I say. 'Nothing to worry about though. Did either of you happen to hear anything last night, scratching from the attic or whatever?'

'Negative,' says Daniel.

'Nope,' says Rachel.

I count on this, love it about them. Once they are asleep at night they still sleep the sleep of the blessed. Nothing wakes them. I have always put music on, even when they were babies; I have put it down to this. Danny has told me that he likes to hear it coming through the floor as he drifts off because then he knows that I am there.

After the school run I unwrap a Mars Bar in the loft and unsheath a fun-size Milky Way in the cupboard under the stairs, because it seems they might be taking succour there too. Sometime before dawn this morning, twenty-past four maybe, perhaps five twenty-five when the luminous hands on the alarm clock were clapping, I was chokered out of sleep by a vicious dream: I was hanging by the neck from an oak the kids climb in woods at the back of the house. I got up to try and wash the dream away with a drink of water and to check the children. Then Evie was on the landing, naked, which she never is, she's always in that robe; and she was like some sort of walking map, creased and pressed with those tracks, lines and hollows you sometimes get when you've clenched and pushed yourself too tight under sleep. 'Can't you hear them now,' she demanded. 'Downstairs, scrambling over the shoes, climbing on the pipes and meters.' I had told her that I couldn't, but I thought that maybe I could. I don't know. We both have these imaginations. I pocket the chocolate wrappers and go out to do a few jobs in town; I want to be amongst people and moving through the streets.

It's not even noon when I get back, but the Milky Way has been crumbed, almost disappeared. 'Fuck me,' I say out loud, 'give Evie's ears their due.'

I head up to our bedroom, but I don't want to return up the ladder I left in position as if inviting them down: down the ladder you come boys, to gobble us up, to gobble us up. I am steeling myself for rats not mice. Somehow it is rats that disappear your kids' sweets in a morning and bang the fuck about in a cupboard under your stairs whilst you are busy dreaming that you're dead. Somehow it is rats that your wife can be bothered to hear when she cannot be bothered to hear you. Fucking rat bastards; come out, come out wherever you are. Now I want to see you. I go straight up. I slap on the light ready to find them; really hoping to see the little fuckers. I am ready to catch the invaders: looting, pillaging, sugar-rushing themselves silly.

But the loft is still, and cold. The air in here is dead; sealed in and sealed out by the preservative on the treated roof timbers. Being in the loft feels like being back in the room at the funeral parlour where they laid out my dead brother in that pine coffin, stained mock-mahogany. He was shrivelled from cancer and the wait for cremation, and would have been fucked off at the last insult of the silly-crimson-satin-cushioning that almost swallowed his body up. The viewing-room was like the coffin itself: a deep-pile red carpet, pine-clad walls and pine-clad pitched-roof ceiling, both stained that same mock-mahogany. I remember how bruised and dried he looked, desiccated; and how *gone*. I remember how alone I felt, almost as if I was dead too. All sense of life beyond the room left me. It was as if the traffic or people on the busy road just outside, and then the roads and streets and fields beyond that, didn't exist. I seemed not to be breathing at all, and yet I wasn't short of breath; and the air in the room was just like the air in this loft. My brother died not long after Evie and I got together. She waited outside in the car when I went in to see his body: she couldn't understand why I wanted to see it, how I could bear to. She was shocked that I got drunk, and laughed a few times, on the day of the funeral. I wish I had stayed in the room for a longer time; that I hadn't rushed away from him, and out of the cold, still room so quickly. I ruffle my hair, maybe trying to shift the thoughts, maybe because my brother used to do this to me when I was little and he, ten years older than me, was the grown-up.

You can tell the rats have enjoyed the Mars Bar. The scalp of chocolate ridges on top is nearly intact but the belly of softer chocolate underneath has been broken through and eaten out. The nougat and toffee dead-flesh-and-goo insides, have been pulled and threaded onto the floor of the loft and you can see where they've been paddled in and licked and licked. I can imagine a couple of rats, on their sides along the length of the chocolate bar, virtually humping it, pedalling the air as they eat and getting as deep as possible into the sweet treat centre, thinking that this is just the best thing they've ever tasted. Fucking joy. Rats for sure. And they're hiding somewhere, or they've fucked off out of it for the time being. Just like they would, I suppose; all of this is fair enough; you're right if you're a rat. I get rid of the ladder and slam shut the hatch. Then I phone the council to see if they still deal with this sort of thing.

I update Rachel and Danny after school as they Fosbury-flop themselves onto the sofa ready for drinks and biscuits.

'Girls and boys, the rat man cometh.'

'What?' says Rachel.

'A man from the council is calling at our house tonight to check for rats.'

'So we have got rats then?' she says.

'Basically, yes. Almost certainly,' I say.

'How do you know?' Rachel again.

'I put some food down after I dropped you off this morning and they ate it up. Too much of it, and too quickly, for it to be mice.'

'Oh,' she says. 'That's horrible. Where are they?'

'Up in the loft. And it seems they can get into the cupboard under the stairs too, so maybe stay out of there. But I haven't gone eyeball to eyeball with them yet. I reckon they'll stay well out of our way so long as they know we're about. Maybe just move with lots of noise; make like elephants for a few days so they know to get clear.' They chuckle at this.

'Can we watch what the man does, Dad?' asks Danny.

'Wouldn't you rather watch a DVD?'

'No. It'd be educational, wouldn't it? Wildlife.'

'I don't want to watch,' says Rachel. 'He probably looks like a rat and loves rats. He probably stinks because he's down sewers all day.'

'Rachel,' I say.

'How can he love rats if he goes about getting them?' says Danny.

'I'll leave it up to you. There won't be much to see anyway. He'll probably just nip in and pop down a bit of poison or whatever.'

'Exactly,' says Danny. 'I can tell the class tomorrow when it's circle time. Or write it in my news and get a star.'

He reminds me of 1970s Action Man: cropped bristly hair and military-smart; the sort of son my father wanted, the sort of guy I wanted to grow up to be when I used to play with Action Man. He's empty-handed but I suppose the stuff is in his van.

'Pest control,' he says. He holds an I.D. up for a second: Mark something or other.

He steps in. I wonder who the guy Evie fancies is, and realise

I've got no idea who she'd go for now.

'I'm Tommy and this is Danny,' I say. 'If a little girl appears, that's Rachel; but I think she's planning to stay in front of the telly because she's not too keen on the idea of rats.'

'That's little girls for you,' he says, 'mine's the same.'

Rachel wouldn't have let him get away with that. I close the front door and we walk through to the breakfast room where the stair cupboard is.

'Thanks for coming out so quickly and so late.'

'It's overtime; my pleasure. Is this the first site then, under the stairs here? Mandy in the office said they'd polished off a Mars or something.'

I open up the cupboard, put the light on, and show the place: next to a hole where the gas pipes come up to meet the meter. I'm glad the crumbs are still there, that they haven't been back already. 'A small Milky Way bar, between ten and twelve this morning, just those few crumbs left.'

'Have you used my chocolate, Dad?' Danny asks.

'Yep, but we've plenty left buddy,' I say.

The rat man gets down on his hands and knees and crawls into the cupboard. He puts his nose down to the skirting boards and sniffs deeply a few times as he makes his way round the cupboard. I daren't look at Danny. We're wired the same way when it comes to what makes us laugh.

The rat man crawls back out, stands up, and gives us his prognosis. 'It's rats not mice. With mice there's usually indicators: droppings and the smell of their urine. Mice drop all the time you see, including where they feed. Rats drop away from the nest and feeding sites. Nest might be near by, might be far away. Often it's under the floorboards: that could be under your house, or the other houses in the terrace.'

'Right,' I say; thinking that we're getting educated, like Danny said.

'It was the loft as well, then?'

'Yes. That was the Mars bar,' I say. 'Similar story, but a bit uglier.'

'Do I need my steps to get up there?'

'There's a ladder that slides down from the hatch,' I say.

'I'll take a look. Then we'll have a chat about what to do. Poison, traps or a bit of both; depending on what you fancy and how many rodents I think you've got. But I won't know that till I get up there and see if they've left me any clues.'

'Clues?' says Danny.

'Yeah, clues. In a space the size of an attic there might be a mess area and a nest to see, if we're lucky.'

'Cool.'

The rat man can't bloodhound any clues, but suspects they're a well established and confident colony because of the high-frequency visiting and the confidence in feeding. Might they have been hiding out in a cavity wall; have we heard any other noises or had any other signs? No matter, he says, once you know you've got them, you can persuade them out.

Evie gets home well after ten. She comes through to the kitchen where I'm waiting for her. She says she's eaten dinner with a colleague before driving the M25. I offer her a glass of wine but she declines. I pour another one for myself anyway, switch off Kirsty Wark starting in on the headlines on the portable telly we keep in the kitchen, take my seat back at the breakfast bar, and tell her our news.

'It's no news to me, Tommy. I told you I heard them. And I don't see why you wasted perfectly good chocolate.' She opens up the cupboard where we keep all the sweet things, breaks off a piece of chocolate from a big bar of Green and Black's, but then puts it back. 'It'll only keep me awake,' she says.

'Well anyway, there's a tray of poison in the cupboard and two up in the loft. The rat man will be back in a week to collect his trays and bag bodies. He predicts they'll be back tonight and that they'll eat the bulk of the bait in one feed. They love the stuff apparently; go mad for the taste of it. It's rat heaven other than the blood starts to thin, and I'm sure you can imagine the rest.'

She gets herself a glass of water from the tap. 'Wouldn't traps have been kinder then?' She gulps it down.

'Hardly ever do a quick, clean break. Instead of the rat's neck snapping they end up caught by their tails or legs or in the middle of their bodies, where they're more flexible apparently.'

'Thanks for that, Tommy.'

'He's known them gnaw through their legs to escape or to drag the trap around with them, carrying on for days until they finally die. People call him back out for the half-dead trapped rats because they haven't the constitution to deal with them themselves. He says that they hiss a lot but that all you need to do is remember you didn't ask them to come into your home, take a deep breath, and knock them on the head.'

'Tommy, what is the matter with you?'

'Danny wanted traps but I didn't fancy it, and didn't think you would either, so that's why I turned his offer of traps down. He did this sniffing like a bloodhound. I think…'

'Danny heard all this?'

'Some of it. He wanted to see what the man did; I think he's old enough now to choose for himself. Rachel chose to stay in the lounge with a DVD. Besides, what's the harm anyway?'

'I'm going to go up to bed, Tommy. I want to fall asleep before they start with that noise again.'

'Oh, shall I come?'

'If you like.'

'I think the rat man secretly loves traps; I bet he thinks poison is cowardly. And the shame is that he hardly gets to use traps because most people don't want them. They'd rather chance a rat being irretrievable, stuck behind walls or in awkward spots, poisoned and slowly rotting. They'd rather chance the stench. But he says it soon goes, that nature, flies and maggots get to work. Then it's just a memory; rats are still everywhere but it's like you've never had them.'

'Tommy, come up to bed. We'll talk about this in the morning if you really must.'

'He went round the outside of the house showing places they could have got in; showed me the places where I could try and block them out. But he says it's a constant chore to make a home rat-proof and you've got to know what you're doing.'

'I'm going to bed, Tommy.'

'They feed and breed all the time and they build up tolerance to the poisons. He says they'll survive when we're long gone. We'll never win the war, only the battle, apparently.'

'Tommy, I really do not want to talk about this now. It's disgusting; them scrambling about just the other side of the ceiling and eating up that poison. I feel sorry for them if that makes you feel any better. Now come on. Come up to bed, get some sleep, and forget about it. By the morning it'll probably all be over.'

By the time she's under the duvet it's too late, they've started up. I can hear the trays scraping on the hardboard floor. Each tray has a dense wax licking-block impregnated with poison. It's supposed to attract the rats and weigh the tray down but it needs to be heavier.

'I take it you can hear,' I say.

'Yes thanks.' She pulls the duvet off her.

On honeymoon we beach-combed shells and called them treasure. We put them in the bath at the hotel. Each time I showered I watched the remains of the life from inside the shells swirl around the bath's floor and get taken down the drain. On the last day of the honeymoon we dried the shells with Evie's hairdryer and shined them on our shirts. The shells sit in a wicker basket on a shelf in our bathroom.

I put my trousers over the door and drop my boxers into the laundry. 'Do you want me inside you, then?'

'Yes, but I don't want you starting with your talk. Now climb in; we'll both feel better for it.'

I think I can hear the rats crunching the granules of poisoned feed, quite apart from the noise of the trays moving. 'Can you hear what I can hear?'

'I'm sure I can and I don't want to talk about that either; now hop in.'

It's the end isn't it, when you're about to fuck to cover over, or maybe even to accompany, the noise of rats eating poison?

'I'm surprised they don't make the trays, that they put the poison in, rat-shaped; to attract them'

'I'm trying not to think about the rats, Tommy.'

I switch off the light and slide in beside her. 'Let's make love then, my girl.'

'Finally. Now take your time, my boy.'

Good. I want to savour and remember. I begin Evie's sequence: turn onto my side to face her, choose a breast, and apply the oh so gentle stroke with the back of my hand, barely glancing and bumping its nipple. Slowly we swell from soft to hard: her teat, my prick; filling with blood. Evie pushes herself up the bed and lifts up her breast; I move my head down and stretch my tongue out to just touch the tip of her nipple, before taking my tongue away again. Her breast quivers and I know to tease it: circling, dabbing, soft-lashing its nipple with the tip and the top and the back of my tongue. When this is done I make to move away and so she pushes her breast into my face, her nipple to my mouth; my sign that she, it, are now ready for the next few minutes. I rub her nipple with my tongue. I paddle, lap, suck and chew. It's cups of warm milk and a feast of soft cookies straight from the oven. How can I love this so much when I was fed from the bottle? But I will have to stop in a moment otherwise she will come; she likes to come only by the cock, her own hand, or a masturbatory push into the mattress.

'Stop, or I'm going to come,' she says.

I let go; letting her nipple out through my teeth and saying a goodbye with a flick of my tongue just as she thinks she's clear. Evie pauses and slows her breathing. I think I can hear the rats tumbling over each other in the cupboard downstairs.

I think of her when we first met: her long, defiant neck; her quick, small eyes that looked everywhere but at you; her quick brain and her flirting. But I found her repellent too: old; grey-skinned; waxy-looking. I thought we'd only do each other harm. But I let her fuck me anyway, after a year of talking-nights, and afterwards I laughed and laughed. I remember how I used to love to smell her breath, and smell and taste, her throat, her neck, her ears. Sweet earth. I remember how I used to love to kiss her, to taste and feel her mouth. Sweet-water cave.

We're still side-by-side, face-to-face. I smooth a hand over her hip and run it down to the soft skin inside the top of her thighs. I can feel the heat from her cunt on my hand. I bet those rats would like to find this cunt; a warm place to rest after they've had their fill. Her back arches. She claws two handfuls of my arse; slides onto my cock. She's soaking and wonderfully warm. She's a bath. I hold her gently in the small of her back and tightly with my hand spread across the cheeks of her arse, feeling her waist move in my arms at the same time. Feeling our stomachs knead together. Fucking is so much better than no fucking for as long as it lasts. I can hear her close, small noises as we move together and apart: the slup of her cunt, and her breath at her mouth.

Her sequence continues: she climbs on top and I finger her arsehole; I want her from behind but she wants me on top so I go on top.

She's not far off the quick pulsing clinging of coming, not far off stretching that neck of hers out and uhrrring those quiet moans of hers that I love to make her make, when I put my face to hers and smell the breath coming from her mouth: it's sweet, warm; that earth I remembered. She pushes my face back so I move it to the side of her head and put my nose into her ear and snuffle the hole and find her close, sweet smell again.

'Tommy,' she says. 'Don't.'

I switch on her bedside light. When her mouth opens to protest I kiss her. Tasting her again is, I don't know, it's the water from that sweet earth; it's as much of her as I can know, and it makes me stop. I take my tongue out of her mouth and put my head onto the pillow beside her. I wanted her, I wanted to find her and for her to be my treasure, I wanted for me to be her treasure; I wanted her to come out to play, I wanted to find her and make her happy. I pull my cock out of her cunt and roll over onto my back, onto my side of the bed so that all I can see is the woodchip-papered ceiling. I chose this woman; she chose me.

'Tommy, what the hell is the matter with you?'

I listen for the rats. Nothing. They've finished their feed. 'I can't hear them, can you?' I say.

'I was just about to come. A whole evening horny and you're on about the fucking rats and sticking your tongue in my mouth. What *is* the matter with you?'

'Why don't you just fuck *him*, Evie?'

'Oh.'

I turn my head to see if she blushes. I don't know why because I don't think I have ever known Evie to blush. Her face is a mask, as ever: ill-tempered-face, her favourite. Even this she turns away; points her mask at her patch of ceiling. I wonder if she can hear the rats; maybe they're having some after-dinner fucking and she can hear with those ears of hers.

I used to want to eat her; lift her skirt and slowly clean and collapse her. Now I'd have to cook her first: wash, dress and cook her. Only then could I eat her flesh. I used to say that we were mammals, just to piss her off, just to point out that we were only animals after all. But she was dead meat; kill. I realise now that that's why I wanted for us to be together. A thing for resurrection.

'It's been like fucking a waxwork, Evie, or a corpse. But I must like fucking dead people; I like fucking you whoever you are. I wanted to bring us back from the dead and I failed. For that I'm sorry.'

'You're just angry.'

'I take it you are leaving. Now that I know; that your good news is out. Now that you have an excuse. Never mind that you're not the only person in this family.'

'I don't know. I want to be free to start the relationship, I suppose.'

'So you haven't started it already then?'

'A bit. I'm sorry. I fell in love, I suppose. I never thought I'd love anybody but now I find that I can. I'm in love with somebody else.'

I start to laugh.

'We haven't done anything. Nothing much. Just talked and kissed.'

I remember again my laughing the first time we went to bed together. I couldn't stop then, and it bothered Evie; she didn't understand my relief and that nothing is funnier than the truth, that the truth always makes me laugh. I can't stop now either.

I get out of the bed and notice that my hard-on has gone but this only makes my ha-ha-ha's come louder. 'What about the children?' I manage to say.

'What?' she says.

'What's that about the children?' says Danny, coming into the room but not knowing yet that anything is wrong. He's not sleepy or confused; he's wide awake and I think he thinks it's morning. He's asking with happy suspicion like he thinks we've been chatting about some treat for him and Rachel, a trip to the zoo at the weekend, or he's discovered that we've got a nice surprise waiting for him, maple syrup pancakes for breakfast.

He starts laughing too. Maybe because he's joining in with me, maybe because he's noticed that we're both naked. Then he spots the chocolate wrappers sticking out a back pocket of my trousers that are hanging over the door. They are making a neat V. For victory? For fuck off? I've no idea which. 'Can I have one?' he asks me.

'Danny,' Evie says.

I'm still laughing but I stop for the breaths to tell him, that we'll go downstairs to get him one in the morning, but that it's just the middle of the night, and that those are just wrappers. He's definitely joining in now; he finds this every bit as funny as I do. And it's going to be a few moments till we're ready to stop, and gasp, and feel the ache in our ribs.

The Wife and the Waitress

Alice Kuipers

W

His girlfriend answered the door wearing a white shirt, a short black skirt, fishnet tights and heels.

'Hello, sir. Welcome to Leila's Restaurant. Have you made a reservation?'

Two candles lit the room. The curtains were drawn and the table was covered in crêpe paper. Pop music played.

He leant to kiss her and she pulled back, shaking her head. Helping him take off his coat, she repeated what she had said, then walked over to his music stand, which she must have brought down from his studio, and tapped a pen on the paper she'd put there.

Grinning, he stepped over to the music stand. 'Yes: I reserved a table.' He saw his name on the sheet of paper. 'That's me there.'

H

The instructions had been on his desk this morning, written on pink card. Our place. 1pm. A table for two.

O

The house was small; the kitchen and living room area was a single room.

She led him to the table, pulled out his chair and tucked it under him. Holding a pad of paper, she asked what he wanted to drink, then rushed into the kitchen and came back with the menu. 'Whoops,' she said.

Teasing her, he asked for a Strawberry Daiquiri and she winked.

'Would a glass of orange juice do, sir? It's on the menu there, look.' She pointed. 'Juice a la casa.' The menu was printed on pink paper with clip art flowers around the edges.

Starter:
Delicate salmon and asparagus with a small bowl of cheese and vegetable soup.

'Sounds good,' he said. He was glad she did not write menus in real life.

She moved like a dancer, although she'd never had lessons. 'You can't talk to me when I'm in the kitchen. You have to pretend you can't see me.'

'You're a very bossy waitress. And I *can* see you.'

Main:
Whole wheat sandwich with British Pork and salad.

'Where's that drink? Slow service—'

He felt her lips on his neck.

Breathing into his ear, she whispered, 'Sorry I'm late, love.' She wore a burgundy dress. Her brunette hair shone in the candlelight. On her fourth finger was a ring. She sat and asked, 'Have you been waiting long?'

He kissed her on the cheek. She sat opposite him.

'Funny, you look a lot like the waitress,' he said.

'Did you order for me? I love this place. The food is always great.'

Brushing a hair from her face, he said, 'No, I haven't ordered yet. The service is slow. I haven't even got my drink.' He looked at his watch.

'I'll have the same as you. Excuse me, I have to go to the bathroom.' She got up from the table.

He began to turn around. She said, 'No. Don't.'

A

Back in the white shirt, she placed his juice before him and took his order. 'Will your companion have the same thing?'

Playing along, he said, 'Yes. She's just in the bathroom, but she'd like the same.'

'Certainly.' She slipped her hand onto his shoulder. 'I have to say, sir – while she's away – you're very attractive.'

He watched her walk back to the kitchen.

'You can't see me, remember?' she said.

R

'Did you order, darling?' She was in the dress again. 'How was work?'

A new song started. It was a love song. The candlelight flickered. He drank his juice. It had a slice of lime in it. He thought of the waitress.

'I love you,' he said. In his pocket, his phone vibrated. He moved his leg.

She leaned over the table and linked her fingers through his. 'It's our wedding anniversary today. Ten years. I know I'm not as energetic as when we first met, and that having children has tired us out. That we never have time for each other, but–'

'Jesus, it's not going to be like that if we get married,' he cut in.

'But I want to say that I love you too.'

He shook his head, laughing, 'This is mad.'

'Excuse me,' she said. 'I need the bathroom again. I think I must have bladder problems.' Her eyes shone.

E

He met Leila when he was in love with someone else. But Leila was keen, and tender, and available. Next thing he knew they lived together and two years had passed. He got her name wrong six times in the first eight months. It made her weep with frustration, but always afterwards she would kiss him softly on the cheek and say, 'I love you.' They said they loved each other as often as they ate dinner. He read once that men fall in love more quickly than women.

After a year, the other girl called and asked him if he was happy. He told her that he was very happy. Thanks for asking. When Leila asked who was on the phone, he didn't lie. He saw her clench her jaw and put his arms round her.

'I love you, Leila,' he said. 'She was beautiful. But so are you.'

Y

In the white shirt, she brought over the food. This time she didn't speak. One of the buttons on the shirt was undone so he could see her lacy bra underneath. The nipple of one breast peeped out. He knew her stomach was toned and flat.

O

Everything was served at the same time.

She must have spent hours on this. He started eating the soup.

'Doesn't the food look good, darling?' she said.

He winked, and said, 'It would be good with cheese.'

She raised one eyebrow. 'Are you sure?'

'Yep.'

She pulled a face. 'I'll run over and ask the waitress for you.' As she stood up, she lifted her dress and pulled it up. In the half-light he saw her tight black knickers. Her birthmark at the top.

The white shirt completely open she leant over and whispered, 'Is everything alright, sir?'

Taking her hand he said, 'I wanted cheese.'

'Your girlfriend has left you again? Silly girl. An attractive man like you.' She climbed over his lap so her legs were spread each side of him. 'I'll get the cheese in a moment.'

'I have a wonderful wife,' he said. She kissed him and opened her mouth; shoved his hand up her skirt. She wore no knickers.

He pushed his finger inside her. 'My wife will be back in a minute.'

U

He'd had a lot of relationships, only a few one-night stands. Maybe 60 breasts, 60 legs, 60 arms, 30 vaginas.

Leila first mentioned getting married after five months. He wrapped his arms around her and looked over the top of her head. He figured he'd have to do it one day: although the words made him want to dive out of an aeroplane, made him want to visit a country he'd never seen before, made him want to walk across a vast expanse of sand. He wanted to do it, he said. He would get there, he said. He loved her.

He found it hard to think of her. As he came he always closed his eyes, imagined women he'd seen walking past. Women he hadn't made love to. When she asked if they could make love without coming, he had to keep his eyes open.

S

The white shirt lay on the floor. His phone vibrated in his pocket again. She was sitting in front of him as wife: in the black dress. They had been talking about his day at work. They had nearly finished the food.

Suddenly Leila said, 'Did you kiss the waitress.'

He looked at her. 'I did kiss the waitress.'

A smile half-moved her lips. 'Did it feel good?'

'No. She made me do it.'

Her jaw tightened, he saw the muscle flex in her cheek. She said, 'Have you finished your main course?'

He reached over to hold her hand. 'What? What's wrong?' She looked away, and he changed the subject. 'So, this is lovely. Thank you. Is there dessert?'

Looking up at him, through her lashes, she teased, 'We could ask the waitress. Or we could go back to my place before you go back to work.'

He looked at his watch and stepped out of role by whispering, 'Does that mean upstairs for ten minutes?'

She nodded.

He let go of her hand, 'I think I'd like to pay the bill and go back to yours.'

Kissing him in that way they had, she murmured, 'Right, I'll go on ahead. Come and join me.'

C

He walked over to the kitchen area and spoke into the silence. 'I'd like to pay.'

She came from the stairs, wearing the white shirt. She offered him her hand. 'You can pay in the bathroom.'

He took it, and she walked him to the toilet, sat him down and unzipped him. On her knees she opened her mouth. It was warm.

Panting, he muttered, 'My wife's waiting for me.'

She sucked harder.

The toilet seat was cold. 'How much will this cost?' he asked.

R

Once Leila asked, hypothetically, if he'd ever slept with a prostitute. The answer left her quiet for some time. 'But,' he told her, 'it was before I met you. I was single. I was lonely.'

E

He stopped just before he came, and pulled up his trousers, 'My wife is waiting.'

She tilted her head to one side. 'As you wish.' It was one of their sayings. Walking out the bathroom, she headed up the stairs.

On the bed, wearing the dress and the knickers, he found her waiting. 'Sorry, it took a while to pay,' he said.

W

He came inside her, his eyes shut. She pulled her dress down.

I

When his phone vibrated for the third time she said, 'It's your phone, babe.'

He pulled away, he said, gently, 'I don't need to answer it.'

She breathed in sharply.

Standing up he said. 'I love *you*, Leila. You know that, right?'

The sunlight in the bedroom made her more naked. She looked away. 'Did you screw the waitress?'

'I love you, Leila. Lunch was great.' He was putting his trousers on, and then his shirt.

She sat up and hugged the sheets round her. 'Give me a kiss.'

'I liked having you as my wife.' He kissed her softly on the cheek. 'I'm getting there.'

Returning his kiss, she said, 'I'll see you when you get home.' And she dressed in her usual jeans and black top, pulled her hair into a ponytail.

N

'Have a good day,' they said to each other at the door. 'Love you.'

G

The air outside was cool. He glanced over his shoulder at the house. Leila was pulling up the curtain. She waved at him.

'I love you,' he mouthed.

Opening the window, she called out, 'Thank you, sir.'

He got into the car. He thought he heard her say, 'Come again.'

?

He smiled, his hand already on his phone.

Bread and Autism

John Carnahan

I meet many of the diagnostic criteria for Asperger's Syndrome, or near-autism, while my son David is farther along the spectrum towards pure autism. My wife Cynthia is not autistic, just nerdy. Very few women are autistic, while each cohort of males since the sixties has been more and more autistic. Cynthia says that men are evolving because the future needs wizards instead of warriors – in other words, we have to live with this. But we can't, so we made a vow on Cynthia's Wicca altar. Holding hands over the candles, we swore that, although David will never be cured, we will still pursue anything that makes him one iota less disabled.

I work the dawn shift at the lab, when there is less random vibration and light to screw up experiments with the Indian corn. Afterwards, I could wait in the parking lot for twenty minutes before I pick up David, but instead I've been entering the warehouse to watch Marjorie Rowe's class. The last place we sent David was secretly doing Holding Therapy and we want to make sure that Marjorie Rowe's Play Therapy is valid. I like how Marjorie can be exasperated in a cool way. She stands with her hands on her hips and her head tilted playfully, and she says It would sure be nice if you did something with your fingers besides jab your forehead, Randy, or I would love to hear you say something besides Out, David. Only one kid notices me sitting on the mattresses near the closet: a squat Korean girl named Lisa who gets mad at the other kids, because she isn't really autistic, in fact she tries to make eye contact with me when she can't get Marjorie Rowe's attention. Marjorie is forming an assembly line of seven-year-olds and David is weaving through the line so he isn't close to Lisa. Each boy in the line picks Lego parts from a plum-coloured bin, adds one new attachment to a Lego Star Wars Imperial Cruiser, and passes it left. It goes to Seth, then Sam, then David – all three have sandy Beatles haircuts because it's less trouble, but Seth and Sam have narrower pixie faces and David's face is more square-jawed. Sam sticks a white-

135

coated doctor Lego on the deck of the cruiser and hands it to David.
David stands still holding the spaceship at arm's length. His brain is
wrestling with the universe. Ever go nuts trying to align a crooked
picture, feel like making it more crooked? Well whatever David adds to
the Lego spaceship must align with a) the crazy-quilt of Lego sockets
and surfaces, b) the boys to his left and right, c) the reflected row of boys
in the mirrored wall, and d) the acoustic ceiling panels crossing his area
diagonally. I don't believe in telepathy but I send David the thought
Don't hate, just think, you're a god when you think. David attaches a
doctor Lego to the deck facing Sam's doctor Lego shoulder-to-shoulder.
Does the white-coated Lego man remind him of the coats we wear in
the cold room at the lab? Why am I sad or is it angry? Goodbye Seth,
goodbye Sam, goodbye Mrs. Rowe, David says coldly. Outside in the hall
he says OUT! OUT! OUHOUT! as a release, and I imitate him tone
for tone. At the video store I leave him strapped in the car, because last
time he got over-stimulated by a loud music video and kicked over a
stack of popcorn boxes. I'd like to kick over some boxes. I'm thinking
DAMN MARJORIE ROWE IF SHE'S PREPARING DAVID FOR
THOSE FACTORIES WHERE RETARDED ADULTS ASSEMBLE
WIDGETS.

The video store is empty. I sweep down the aisle between Comedy and
Thriller eyeballing the alphabetized titles left and right. Mistakes were
made. I move *The Matrix* from T back to M and *The Rapture* from
Romance back to Science Fiction/Horror. No, this would not be a
night for *The Rapture*. Random DVDs wash in and out of the store and
I sift 'em and sort 'em like a prospector. The right disk guarantees the
whole evening. Here is *The Sixth Sense* turned picture-outwards for
display. My pants are loose enough that I can reach in and scratch my
hip as I examine the disk. The boy sees ghosts and the guy telling the
story is really a ghost, too – surprise! Defects of *The Sixth Sense*: too
popular with typicals, re-hash of *Jacob's Ladder* which re-re-hashed *An
Occurrence at Owl Creek Bridge*. Cynthia doesn't like horror movies
although she likes horror novels because she can control the experience,
she says. Could start up the did-I-see-a-ghost argument again. Merits of
The Sixth Sense: it's supposed to be subtle, it's one of the few fantasy
movies we might like and haven't seen, and it's been on video too long
to be a mundane choice. Somebody in the store likes it. Now I've
smudged the case with my fingertips. Choose, I tell myself, Cynthia will

adjust. I executive-march up to the clerk and disk, dollars, demagnetized, I escape.

The first shot of the movie has a fisheye view of an urban park that's shaped like a coffin. Duh. I like this, Cynthia says. Glad, I say, passing her the bowl of Oreos. A table between our recliners blocks David from seeing the movie while he sits on the floor behind us with a game in his lap and a Cherry Big Gulp at his side. Sometimes he'll watch nature shows, but Hollywood movies with their parade of facial expressions get on David's nerves. He still wants to be near us while we watch them and sometimes we can hear him pressing buttons then exhaling when he completes a row of Tetris. On the TV screen Cole, the little boy who interacts with ghosts, sits at the kitchen table while his mom goes in another room. The camera stays on her while she rummages around a linen closet. Crash! Back in the kitchen, every drawer and cupboard has been opened by the ghosts, and Cole is just sitting there with his palms flat on the table. Mom thinks he did it. Does that remind you of your mother? Cynthia asks. Not really, I say, I think the movie is saying that everything happens when you turn your back. The mother looked away, the camera looked away, and then – surprise! Speaking of kitchens, Cynthia says, I would like some of the chicken with a little potato salad. We both say Out before we pause the DVD. Thanks, husband, Cynthia says when I return with the plate of food. You're welcome I say loudly. On the paused DVD Cole is wearing a suit and tie for school and looking up at his mother with big eyes. Look at the little gentleman, Cynthia points with her fork, like he's taking her out on a date. He's dressed for Catholic school, that's why like that, I say, but what good is Catholic school if you see ghosts? Cynthia un-pauses the disc, Cole goes into another room to talk with Bruce Willis, who is supposed to be a child psychiatrist but is really another ghost. Cole's autistic, I say. Unh-uh, Cynthia says, he's like a fantasy of a perfect kid who's sweet and quiet. They're not going to make a movie about a single mom with a real autistic kid. On the screen Cole turns his head to the wall while Bruce Willis tries to talk to him. I say LOOK, HE'S CONTROLLING STIMULI. HE'S AUTISTIC. Cynthia says How much do you need to be right about that? Ninety-five per cent, I say. Okay, she says, we'll try it that he's autistic.

Out of the depths I cry to thee O Lord – said in the church scene –

Bruce Willis has arrived because the mother and son prayed – the movie's encouraging women to be Christians. I like that it turned out to be a woman, Cynthia says. His mother? I ask. No, silly, the rich woman poisoned her daughter and the daughter's ghost shows Cole whodunnit, in the funeral home scene – I like it that they showed a woman abusing her kid instead of always the man. I shake my head. I don't think Cynthia sees that Cole is a symbol of developmentally disabled kids, and the movie says God will fix it. Cole is starting to smile a lot – it's going to end soon, I say. Cynthia says, He'll keep helping the ghosts go back to the afterlife. He'll be the lost and found of lost souls. He's a good wizard. Out, I say as the coffin-shaped park fills the screen again. Ouhout, Cynthia says, looking back at David. NEVER! David shrieks. NO, I say. NO, Cynthia says, How dare you? We don't yell at you when you say Out. I say The movie's OVER, David! I notice that I'm panting. Was David watching the movie?

David is on his third viewing of The Sixth Sense. He doesn't watch the whole movie, just the scenes with Cole. He has figured out how to work the DVD remote by himself. I should look at my watch, but I don't want this to end. I know how it feels to suddenly understand how to work a machine. Cynthia and I watch him through the bedroom door. Cynthia says, He's watching their faces, Larry, oh my God. This has something to do with your ghost. You do have a ghost, do you accept it now? I say I NEVER COMPLETELY DENIED IT. REMEMBER ME LAST WEEK SAYING I FELT HAUNTED WHEN DAVID HANGS AROUND MY ELBOW, LIKE AT BREAKFAST? HOW IT REMINDED ME OF...?

Make my son Cole, make me Bruce Willis – I try to sound funny and suave while Cynthia watches us and drinks cola. David, listen; oh, back of David's neck, I've got a story. David's ear turns to me, face to the wall, concentrating on the sounds of my words. David's sperm whale face scared us when he was a baby, then we learned that it means concentration. Okay, David, when I was eleven I saw a ghost in a cabin in the Sierras. My parents had been fighting so my dad and my sister were in a separate room. My mother and I were asleep. It was dark. A voice woke me up. A little girl's voice where there should be no little girl – an emergency voice. Bread, bread. That's what I heard. Bread, bread. I saw her outline beside me in the dark, just a black shape. She smelled like mud. I couldn't always decode words and I was scared why she kept saying Bread. My mother woke up. Mom had a lighter, like the ones we use to light candles but bigger. I saw a big shadow in the room, like a tall man, and my mother screamed. My father came in with a flashlight and there were no ghosts. My mother said I woke her up with a crazy nightmare because I had been reading a science fiction book. My dad hit me and threw away the book. My mother went to sleep in the other room and I had to spend the night alone. I can't explain it, but I fell asleep. If there were ghosts, I wasn't afraid of them. I was afraid of my family all the way home. They blamed me for something. I decided that I was really a ghost inside but I couldn't tell anybody. I didn't know yet that I was autistic, I thought I was a ghost searching for its purpose on earth. Like the way the ghosts in the movie keep doing the same things until Cole helps them. When I met your mother we had a long talk about it – from her recliner Cynthia says It's true, David, you're finding out about us – and she helped me to know that it was real. That I did see a real ghost. That seeing a ghost helped me be a functioning autistic. Maybe the real ghost put a switch in my head to let me choose to be autistic or not sometimes. It's okay to be autistic, but have you ever wanted to be not-autistic for a few hours a week? Be like someone else? Would you like that? David nods. Would you like to see a real ghost? David nods. Good agreeing, I say.

I've called in sick; the sun rises for us today. Carloads of neurotypical children and parents and ski racks pass us and Cynthia rubs my shoulders from the back seat. David, I say, let's look for out-of-state plates. I show David what one looks like and how he can tap on the dashboard to count them. Lightly, Cynthia says, laying down so she can read. East of Oakdale the highway narrows to two lanes. I have to watch the oncoming cars so I can't always see the out-of-state plates before David, and they're surprisingly rare; has everyone moved to California? David isn't playing. Sometimes he notices a deserted barn and nods his head four times rapidly and I wonder if he sees a ghost, or if I am just fooling myself with a new theory about his behavior, like before when it was all nutrition. He is so dazed by the car trip, the lack of sleep, the way Cynthia and I are acting. I say his favorite words: Out, never, toilet, black, hungry, yes, no. He repeats them after me. Seven out of maybe seven thousand words we've tried to teach him registered in his brain like seven digits of the combination of a lock.

Look, we're entering a volcano, Cynthia says. She sits up in the back seat and we can feel her weight shift to the driver's side of the Honda. Cynthia says This whole valley used to be a caldera, that's why you see lava sticking up all over the hills. See how the ranchers used lava rocks to make a fence for their cows? That part of the rim over there is called Table Mountain. Hey Larry, Cynthia says to me, we have to stop at a supermarket or something in Jamestown. I nod. We prowl down Main Street, finding mostly antique shops; David stares up at the balconies and attic windows of the old-time houses. At Tom's Mountain Market twenty per cent of the fluorescent lights have burned out. There are four checkout stands with outdated tabloids, old snack foods and unpopular cigarettes, and only one clerk, an old Chinese lady with a daffodil hanging out of her apron. We get wheat bread, PB&J for David, salami and cheese for ourselves, lots of Sprite, and Oreos and microbrews to seduce – Cynthia says that, seduce – the camp caretaker. I buy a separate bag of goodies from the dry goods section: index cards, notebooks and pens, tracing paper and charcoal, a pocket telescope, pocket flashlights, batteries, a can of phosphorescent Silly String. I carry that bag and Cynthia takes the two big bags of groceries. Damn it, the exit turnstile, which is a long distance from the checkout stand, won't turn to let us leave. Metal spokes stronger than man, I say, pushing against the frozen wheel, then I gingerly climb over the turnstile and Cynthia hands me the bags. Back at the checkout stand a tall skier buying rock-salt watches us through her aviator sunglasses. There is a secret door, I tell Cynthia. To the right Cynthia is blocked by a row of shelves connected to the turnstiles, like a customer fence, which she explores from her side and I explore from mine. Secret door behind bookcase, she suggests, but the display of magazines is too heavy for us to move; however, a small rack of trail mix and dried fruit moves aside easily. The exit's over there you fools, the skier says. That pocket telescope I got is only ten times magnification, but it's light, I tell Cynthia, maybe we can go up on a hill and see the Leonid meteors. Cynthia says We can see Mars in Scorpio, I'll bet. We can signal the mothership to beam us up. Back in the car David is resting with his front teeth against the dashboard, like he fell asleep biting it. He blinks and smiles when I open the door.

David seems fascinated by the rows of pines that look like saw-teeth from a distance; I think he's watching them change colour as the sun goes behind the ridge. When he's tired, the urgency drains out of his face except for his eyes, which are still active but not interactive, as Marjorie Rowe would say. David senses that Cynthia and I are lost. The Yahoo map doesn't really show the roads in the Stanislaus National Forest. When I came here before, my parents fought constantly over something about the Shell credit card; I didn't understand it, but I have a strong picture of them arguing in profile against the blue sky. Cynthia and I are not fighting over the directions, just trying to solve the problem – who needs to yell? We're friends. It's dark now and we are descending into a canyon by a series of switchbacks on a gravel road. I recognize the thundering under the tyres, the way the car seems to coast on the gravel. This is it, I say, My God, we're really here. Okay, Cynthia says, I'm waking up. I say When I was a kid, I thought we were going to stay in an Abe Lincoln-looking cabin, but over this rise you'll see they're more like barracks. There they are. We roll over a plank bridge, into a dirt street between two rows of dark army-type sheds made of green boards. A white van with a light on in the back must belong to the caretaker. Cynthia goes to find him while I help David use the toilet. David's shoulder is soft in my hand but as soon as I pull him out of the car he starts to twist away from me. Look at it, I say, pine needles everywhere. It's a messy place, all right. Okay, David, toilet. Toilet. This way, now. Usually we don't stay in the bathroom with David but I need to distract him because he's never been in a camp toilet before. At least it's more cold and black than hot and full of flies. I see dead people, I say to get David's attention. Nev-er, he says, meaning he can't shit. I stand with my back to him, inhaling clean air from the cracks in the door. I say You know how we go in the parking lot and make the fireworks chain? I want David to forget the camp toilet and instead picture laying out small combustibles and explosives I've brought home from the lab so that they ignite each other in a row. David loves arranging the fireworks chain so much that words like fireworks and fuse over-stimulate him. I say As soon as you're done we'll move into the cabin and call that the fuse, fsst, the fuse goes to the caretaker like firecrackers, then it's a double fuse fsssst back to the cabin, like when we make a double fountain. But we have to lay the fuse out first, y'know. The ghost is like a fountain, David. Yeah, a ghost must be like combustion, plasma that releases its heat and then it's gone for a while. I hear David's turds splash the bottom of the pit, six feet underground. When we return to the cabins Cynthia is being hugged by the camp caretaker who hangs off her like a chimp. Cynthia says Ben, this is my husband Larry. Larry, I was telling Ben some of our disability issues. David whimpers and begins to writhe again because Ben is a rickety old man with long white dreadlocks, a tennis visor, and foul jeans held together by a safety pin.

This is not going to work. This is not going to work. The fucking CABIN has been subdivided into two cabins. It's not the cabin from my imagination anymore. There are no more beds, just a stack of folding cots, like lawn chairs. I tell Ben that BEFORE it was two rooms, and my father and sister stayed in the other one. Ben says Well, I guess they partitioned it, they thought they could make more money that way. Ben drinks from the Anchor Steam we gave him. From the way he looks at the bottle, I think Ben's struggling with alcoholism. Have your beer, Cynthia tells me, We'll still be in the room where you saw the ghost, right?

The four of us sit on a picnic bench around a red kerosene lantern. David notices when I drink, then he goes back to watching the swarm of gnats over the centre of the bench. Yes, there is a ghost in that cabin, maybe more than one, Ben says. Myself I've seen the door open after I've locked it and furniture moved around inside. Heard a loud bang in there at night, when it was empty. Maybe it goes way back to when this was Miwok territory. Now the Miwok braves would – Ben pushes his right index finger through a tube formed by his left fingers – with absolutely anything. Romance an old stump, or a dog, they would do that. Because the Miwok think every rock and animal speaks Miwok, so they'd talk to them the way you would a woman. This is the myth, you know. Up at Lake Annie a Miwok boy said to the lake, you know, Hey, watcha doin'? No answer, but he kept askin'. Finally the lake said Here I am, take me. So he did. They had two daughters, one that was this creek here, one that was a normal human. Pretty soon the human daughter got her period and had to leave. Went over the ridge to Miwok Village, human all too human. You can see the grinding stones there. Um, the Miwok called this Talking Creek because they could hear the creek calling for her sister. Now it's called Peabody Creek because this became the Peabody Ranch, after the Miwok. But maybe you can hear that creek talking some nights. Maybe. Can your son understand anything I'm saying? Yes, Cynthia says, sure. We all want to hear about the ghost. He's autistic, I say, we both are. He won't hear things neurotypically. He wouldn't hear the creek talking. He might hear the creek as, well, an infostream, like numbers rising and falling. Listen. Hear how the creek's like information, like on, off, on, off? Ben tries to meet David's eyes, then goes back to his beer. Ben asks, He's shy? He looks ornery but he's really shy? I say Sort of. Ben says Well, still waters run deep, they say. Him smart cookie. Does he like scary stories? Cynthia and I both nod.

Well this used to be a logging camp after old Peabody sold the ranch to the Hunnicut brothers, around when the dirt highway came in, 1927. To say about the Hunnicut brothers, Jackson and Frank, they were a pair of walking heart attacks. They were with the same investors that made the O'Shaughnessey reservoir. Oh, Christ, what a place this logging camp would've been. Would have been? Cynthia asks. Well I wasn't around then, Ben says, but I've seen plenty like it. Little houses with mud paths between 'em, kids running around naked, fights every Saturday night, Indians, Blacks, Chinamen, every kind of knave in this place. You're a sissy if you don't have an axe on your shoulder, it's like that. Now, they say no American ever starved to death in the depression. True, I say, The idea that people starved is liberal propaganda. Maybe, Ben says, But this one family starved, hear me out. They were Basques. The father, he was a big man with a black moustache. He had been a shepherd. He liked to drink. The mother was very religious – Catholic. She barely spoke English. They had a girl, a little younger than your boy here. All day the father would be out working, and the mother would be home reading the Bible to her little girl. The Indians used to scare the mother by telling her el diablo comes out of the creek at night, so, she wouldn't let her daughter go past the cabins. Her daughter might've been about your age, she would've liked to explore those woods. You might like that. I was quiet when I was a boy, too, and now I prefer it out here by myself. But you've gotta be alert, out in these woods. Alert. Anyway, the mother and the daughter hardly left this cabin. Two years, three years, all the money they make goes back into the company store, which is gone now, it's just a foundation back up the road a bit. Everything they have, the father drinks away. He gets real mean. Wanders around talking to himself in Basque.

Basque is related to no known language, I say. Is that right, Ben says, anyway around 1932 Jackson Hunnicut, the owner, decides to close up shop. Bank failure. That was one of the worst winters on record.

Everyone had to leave the camp, but the Basque family stayed on. Now this part I heard this from Richard Hunnicut, Jackson's boy. This Richard, he owned all that land above the Phoenix reservoir. You drove past his land as you came up here. He died three years ago. Ol' Land Baron Dick was just a boy when he went with his dad to tell the Basque family to leave. The daughter was sick, maybe that's why they didn't want to travel. Richard Hunnicut says that the daughter was begging for food. The mother just stayed in the bed, under the covers. Richard thought at the time she might be dead. The father was drunk, of course; he tried to throw a punch when old man Hunnicut wouldn't give them anything, but old man Hunnicut had a thirty-aught-six and he just told the father to go to hell. Stay there and freeze for all I give a damn. So there they were, the mother all sick under a pile of blankets, the father drunk, the daughter confused, and old Hunnicut just watchin' 'em drown and teaching that attitude to his boy. But just as the Hunnicuts were driving off the mother came running up and got in their truck. She had run out on her husband. She left her daughter? Cynthia asks. Yes, she did. What happened to her? I don't know. She might've wound up at the whorehouse in Jamestown. Ben pauses. Women can be worse than men, Cynthia says. Indeed indeed, Ben says, anyway, winter came and went and the whole place was snowed under. When the Hunnicuts came back in March to look the place over, first thing they saw was two coyotes sitting on the front step of that cabin. Just sitting there like pets at the door, didn't run off when men approached until somebody threw a rock at them. The other thing was the window. Just covered with flies. Just black with flies. As for what was inside, old man Hunnicut would never talk about it. The man and his daughter were dead, I assume. As for ghosts, personally I believe that when you die needing something everyone should have, like food, you stick around for what you didn't get in life.

Cynthia looks at her notes. She says It seems to me that the little girl asked Jackson Hunnicut for bread, but he ignored her. I'm seeing Jackson Hunnicut as a tough rancher with a fur-lined leather coat and a black cowboy hat. And a gun in his hand, and a snarl on his face. His son Richard is kind of pudgy and all bundled up in wool. Naturally, the little girl asked the son for bread. Now what did the son do? He was probably stressed out. I know, I was always afraid of poor people who asked my parents for things. Maybe he couldn't answer. So maybe her ghost keeps trying to ask little boys? Doesn't that make sense, Larry?

You got that thick voice like a retard, but you're sure not retarded, Ben says. He's looking up at me with wet eyes and beer breath. He laughs when I tell him that he, too, has a thick voice at this point. We have been looking at the sky full of stars. David prefers looking at stars through the pocket telescope because it's less chaotic. I say Autistics are more often geniuses than idiots. Einstein would be diagnosed as autistic if he were around today. Ben says Einstein, what a hero. Ben clamps his hand on David's neck; David whines loudly and I feel annoyed because some people try to break down autism by being obviously superfriendly. Cynthia asks him, Will you be okay going home? Hell yes, he says. You take care of your woman and your boy, Larry. You'll be all right. Cynthia and I stand together at the edge of camp, listening to Ben's tyres on the gravel and his gears climbing higher until we are satisfied that he has left the canyon. Cynthia says, Wasn't he going to leave us his cell number? We start to feel cold so we go back to the cabin. One of the grocery bags is tipped over, spilling cookie wrappers. The sight halts Cynthia in the doorway, lantern in hand. I say I probably knocked it over getting the telescope. I was feeling around in pitch darkness. Cynthia nods, but we have to stand the sack upright before we can do anything else, even though we are freezing. Sleeping bags, Cynthia urges. We don't bother with the folding cots. Are we safer inside or out, will David wander off in the dark, is the ghost hateful, should I build a fire, do I know how to build a fire, is it okay to breathe the kerosene fumes, it's taken me years to learn what worries me and years more to learn not to say it. David won't cuddle with us, instead he faces the ceiling and thrashes inside his sleeping bag to warm it up.

He likes you, Cynthia says. Who? Ben, Ben who left at ten. I say Oh. She says Now that it's dark does the cabin seem more like it was before? I say Yes. That window — I went to sleep staring at it because I was afraid of it. I was reading Lloyd Alexander's The Black Cauldron and my sister was reading a book about the Manson Family with a picture of Manson's face on it. I was afraid that I would see Manson's face in that window. There was a tree limb in the window, I'm certain. The creek seemed noisier then, that was another thing keeping me awake, that babbling brook. Now I see there's a lot of stumps around the cabins like it's been logged or burned and the creek is quieter because it's in flood. The

ground and the trees are wet. Cynthia asks Was it this cold? I can see my
breath like Cole in The Sixth Sense when he was about to see a ghost.
I say It's cold inside because we're in the shadow of the canyon walls all
day. Not much light. Cynthia says Well, let's get started. As I crawl around
on my knees sticking candles on the floor for our ritual, I pretend that
I'm Ben when he crawled in and out of his van showing us his treasures.
I say That's a bag of Miwok herbs that can cure cancer, don't open it! I
stick the fourth white candle to the floor in a puddle of liquid wax. I say
This is a gun that belonged to Joaquin Murietta, don't handle it! I stick
down the fifth and final candle. Cynthia laughs. You're pretty hyper, she
says, Let's stand and centre ourselves before we walk the circle. Her hands
grip mine forcefully which means, don't resist. In fact, I suddenly have
nothing in mind. We hold hands over David as we walk around him.
David sleeps like a foetus. Let the power of another world heal us, we
say. I see our shadows wheeling around the walls. Cynthia's breath has its
own shadow. Usually we watch the candles to see if a flame bends left or
right, but tonight they just bend with us when we walk, and sit upright
when we sit. I watch the candles burn down. Are you awake, husband?
Yes, I say, I'm not sleepy at all. She says You're so quiet, do you sense
something? I say I don't know, I'm happy. We're here, not the ghosts,
that's what I feel. We're together. She says I'm really glad we came, then.
But I think I'm too tired. We need to go to bed – you've been awake
since yesterday. Out, I say, blowing out the first candle. Out, Cynthia says,
blowing out the second. I blow out the third, Cynthia blows out the
fourth. I blow out the fifth and we get into our sleeping bags with the
lantern between us. We say Out together and extinguish the lantern and
a big swirl of wax and kerosene gets up my nose. Cynthia says Tomorrow
night we'll be home. She's touching my ear. Her huge hand weighs
nothing. I feel lucky. I think I might not have Asperger's Syndrome.

I pretend that the room we are in is a ship that will travel to Alpha
Centuari. All the rules of nature are obeyed. The ship uses an ion drive
and travels below the speed of light. It will take us five generations to
reach Alpha Centuari. Inside the ship is bare and plain with ribs showing
like the hold of a 747. I have designed the drive, the environmental
systems, the society. We need genetic diversity. Ben's hugging Cynthia so
much could be attraction, among other things. By the time Ben and
Cynthia have a daughter, we have made cave paintings on the walls of
our ship. We will dance around fires inside the ship. No gods, but there

will be rituals to mark the passage of time. Society will evolve from a few external conditions, like having stuff hidden around the ship to encourage exploration and competition. That can be how you allocate resources; for example, some vital equipment might be sealed in canisters that only open when they are moved away from the ship, or better, they open to a combination based on how the stars look from a point away from the ship and midway along its course – you have to go out and make that observation, or no new tungsten filaments. That would keep the spirit of exploration alive. Hermit Ben would die first and be launched into space with country music. Cynthia would die next. Then I would die, then David would grow old and die amongst his children, conceived by artificial insemination if necessary. None of our descendants would be autistic because whatever they are is the norm. They will stand on an alien beach under a triple sun and remember those who passed on the long voyage. Bagpipes in the infra-rainbow. A tear runs down my cheek. Bagpipes in the red and blue light. But what about the dead? Will there be ghosts? A starship filling up with ghosts? It sounds wrong. Ghosts and space seem immiscible like oil and water. What happens to the behaviour-echo or whatever that lingers after death? To the ghosts who say the same name or climb the same staircase night after night? Maybe they live on as stored images. Everyone being audio and video recorded all the time removes the need for playback as ghosts. This solution excites me. We can meet the ghost requirement by information storage and retrieval. Ghosts, did you hear that?

Cynthia is snoring. A few raindrops hit the window, then a shower falls all over the canyon like background radiation. I think there's a voice coming through the rain. I listen for a soft and distant girl's voice; it might be outside the cabin, or inside it, or maybe on the roof where the rain is hitting. NO BREAD, David screams. I can locate his white pyjamas, he's up, he's walking in the far corner. NO BREAD he screams and stomps his feet. His voice is breaking. I'm out of my sleeping bag, I'm standing, but I don't know what to do. NEVER NEVER NEVER NEVER. Cynthia rolls over and aims a flashlight at David: he is marching in place in the corner of the room, stamping his feet in time to NO BREAD. David sees the ghost! I don't want Cynthia interfering and that means pushing her hand and the flashlight down with my outstretched foot, but Cynthia is starting to rise to get David and instead I kick her full in the face, and she cries Oh and falls on her butt. Then my foot comes down on the loaf of bread I had placed near David's sleeping bag. The flashlight breaks on the floor. I hear half-syllables of murmured names everywhere. Get away from me, Cynthia says and pushes me aside. She falls over some bags and then the door opens. NO BREAD. I see rain in the faint doorway; I can't believe Cynthia is gone. I scream as loud as I can. Screaming until my throat aches, clears the room. David is silent. The rain no longer has words hidden in it. I pick up David and he tries to thwart me by arching his legs and slumping his head; we cross the doorway leaning left and right, pausing every third step for balance. I shut the car door. David is in the car. I shut the trunk. I am standing in the woods with a highway flare calling Cynthia!

I'M SORRY I HIT YOU. MY LEG JUST WENT FLUH. Cynthia raises her face out of the creek to reply. I can't hear her over the rain but I am relieved that she can move. She is forty feet from the cabin, face-down on the bank with her hair in the water. With the rain and the red light dripping from my flare she looks like a pink boulder beside the creek, and I have passed her twice calling her name. I crouch beside her. The face is soapy with a black stone from the creek held against the nose with bloody fingers. It must be Cynthia's face but it seems like a mask. I say Cynthia? She says Yes, it's me. I'm okay. I wanted to wash and I had a tooth come out. S'okay, I can take a few knocks. She turns away from me again. I prod her and point out that the creek is rising, we need to get her to a hospital, David is waiting in the car. My voice sounds soft, not urgent. I'm scared. I could barely carry David; I can't move 347 pounds of Cynthia up the bank. I lay down and sidle closer until she flinches. Water runs through our hair into the creek under our faces. I drink from the creek. I say Did you hear the ghost? She says No, sorry, I did hear David say Bread though. She turns her face from me. I say It is nice here. But it's rising, look, that little white rock is gone. Cynthia says All right, let's go.

She wobbles; she would have more balance if she didn't keep the rock pressed on her face. I say Be Xena, and I pull her free arm over my shoulder. I try to lead her up the creek-bed diagonally so we don't slip back, but each step forward sinks us a foot toward the creek. Near the top her weight goes dead behind me and my vision blackens. I'm going to fly into blackness. We fall back several feet and crawl the remaining distance grabbing roots to pull ourselves up. Cynthia drips with mud. At the rim I leave her gasping on a wide flat stump while I go for David. I can't look back at her; I have to hurry before the torch fizzles out. I pass our cabin with its open doorway and worry that David is inside – I forgot to strap him in the car, so he could be in the cabin or in the trees. No, he wouldn't, that's just me freaking out. Furious rain is bouncing off the car. The car door opens an inch and then stops. I yell DAVID and pull hard with my whole weight but it won't open; I see pinprick lights from the effort. I try the rear door, then the doors on the other side hoping one of them will open more than an inch. The windows are opaque and streaming with water. Some kind of power holds all four doors shut from inside. Is there a God, too, who can help me? I find a twenty-pound rock and hurl it at the door window. It bounces off, so I fling it again. Then I remember that this is the passenger side and I might hurt David by breaking the window, so I return to the driver's side. But what if I have scared him over to the driver's side? I kick the door twice to warn him and them bring the rock down on the window. Again. Again. Again and it breaks. I see the whites of David's eyes from the back seat. He's sitting with his hands at his sides. He has barricaded himself inside the car by looping the shoulder-straps through the interior door handles. He watches me undo the straps, motionless, grunting with displeasure when I elbow him aside to clear the back seat for Cynthia. I yell USE YOUR BRAIN TO HELP. JUST ONCE. I whisper Fuck you then David. The engine starts, the headlights work. We rumble along the creek-side and a big fallen limb passes under the whole length of the car, halting us for a second as I start to cry. Then the back tyres roll off the limb. I say I'm sorry that I said that David because I really believe you are always trying in your way to make things right. You love us. Cynthia stumbles into the headlights still holding the rock against her nose.

We climb the stream of white gravel under the headlights. My left arm is freezing and drenched from the broken window and my right arm is getting toasted by the heater. Sometimes the headlights lose the road and jab into the rainy air of the canyon, then I swerve right and find the road again. There's a turn every hundred and fifty yards or so and each turn is equally sharp, so I can blindly anticipate them, that's the secret. In the back seat Cynthia and David are both asleep and piled up against the left-hand door; Cynthia is caked with muck and there's a black blotch in the middle of her face. The gravel road crests the rim and then dumps us onto an abandoned highway where I turn right again, why not. I give the back seat a second look. Yes – David cradles Cynthia; his hand rests on her forehead thus David is protecting another person. Thank you, I say out loud, but not loud enough to wake them. What if they both hate me when they wake up, what if David is not really better? What if seeing a ghost makes you more autistic? What if I was normal before I came here? We have gone off the road onto a shoulder where I stop the car short of hitting some trees. I'm going to black out. It might be best to wait here a few hours. Up the shoulder I can see three redwoods with some kind of light spreading between them. The light is too local to be dawn. It doesn't move so it can't be headlights from another car. Naturally Cynthia and David won't wake up and see the three pines with white lights between them. It's one of those mysteries in the woods I wish I never saw because seeing them puts you alone. I say Thanks again as I rest my head on the steering wheel. I feel grateful, but I feel used, too.

Okay, Cynthia says, Return to the Ghost Cabin Six Months Later, A Wrightson Family Film. The camera zooms on her talking mouth then quickly zooms back to frame her face. I don't know whether David shot that, or I did. For autistics it's hard to find the right angle to see a face; we're like people who have to walk 360 degrees around a statue before we decide what it's about. On the video clip Cynthia says You will note that there is still junk on the floor, just the way we left it. The camera pans across our sleeping bags. From off-camera I say Because it got rained out after we left and Ben didn't come clean it up. That's right, Cynthia says. I say Because nobody can find Ben. Right, Cynthia says. The clip ends. David locates the next clip from the drop-down menu and pulls it into the playing area. His nose is two inches from the computer screen. We're trying to finish the editing before Cynthia gets back from her mother's. The next clip has David standing in the middle of the cabin holding a loaf of OroWheat. From off-camera Cynthia says What is that, David? David smiles, stamps his foot and says NO BREAD. Cynthia says But what is it, David? David stands smiling for a long time. Cynthia says You look like a gangster when you smile. David shifts his weight and my eyes wander over the wallboards behind him. I like the foggy grey light from the window; it gives the wallboards a raw, evil texture. Finally David shouts BREAD. Yes bread, Cynthia says off-screen, As you can see one of us stepped on this loaf when we ran away from the ghost, but it is otherwise intact. No mice have tried to chew through the wrapper in all this time. The clip ends. I try to show David how to shorten the clip but he keeps trying to get ahead of me. Okay, I say, You do it. Move the cutting tool so that it all starts when you say BREAD. David moves the cutting tool to the left of the BREAD soundwave. He's super intense like a real movie editor. HE IS NOT A GHOST.

Heisenberg's Uncertainty

Gabriella Reed

Chloe was standing in the front yard when I got to her house. She had a crushed black-eyed susan under her foot and a look like she didn't know what to do with her hands. Yellow police ribbon was strung over top of her hedge, and in a box around the neighbour's house. Lucky it was near Easter time, made it almost festive. All the flags flapping outside people's doors and the yellow ribbon in the sun.

'Chloe.' I had to step in front of her on the daisies before she'd notice me. 'I saw on the news. God. You know they interviewed Helen across the way? Should've seen you, standing right here and all.'

'FOX-4?' she asked.

'CBS-12. FOX is still on the game. Playoffs, you know.'

'Oh.'

'Sheezus, Chlo, you look like hell.' Why they chose Helen, I was thinking. 'Let's get you inside, okay?' I pulled her out of the flowerbed.

'They were under the porch, Mary Jane,' she said. Nodded at where all the cameras were trained, all the cops were standing around just so to get their faces into a shot. 'That's where he buried the,' hell, she was going to start crying right there, 'the bodies. The whole family. Oh, Lord.'

'Lord's got nothing to do with a thing like this. Come on, now, we'll put on some coffee.'

In the kitchen we turned on the TV and muted the sound. Behind Sheri Kernopolis from CBS-12 was the taped-off neighbour's house and half of Chloe's. In the way back you could see the kitchen window, but not us inside.

I poured some beans into the grinder. She had a good one – quiet enough you could talk over it.

'They arrested him at work, news said. Did you know he worked at the mall?'

'No,' she said.

'The other one, one on the south side of town. In the food court. Christ, I'm glad I never ate there. You imagine? Christ.' Beans were done. 'Chloe? Coffee'll be on in a second, you alright?'

'I'm alright,' she said. She was looking at her hands on the countertop as if they might run away from her.

'Oughta sit down,' I told her.

'I lived here.' She didn't sit down, 'I lived here my whole life, you know? This was my parent's house.'

'I know.'

'When I was just a girl. You remember – I wasn't especially a pretty girl.' I did remember and pretended to disagree. Her hair had been all stringy and it took a while for her to grow into that nose. 'Anyhow, I was a homely little thing and knew it. And he, one day I was getting home from school and he was sitting on his front porch and waved hi. He called me 'sweetheart'. From his porch.'

'Sheez, Chloe. That's creepifying. Do you think he…? Sheezus. You're probably lucky to be alive. Thank God, huh? Christ.'

'I guess. Yeah.'

I could see she had more to say, but, hell, what more can you say when shit like this happens? The guy was a psycho.

I put some cheerful in my voice and asked, 'You found a present yet? Not that you got to tell me what it is, of course.' She looked up.

'What?' she asked.

'For the baby shower? Tuesday?'

'Mmm,' she said, though not like she'd understood a word.

I shut off the television and we could hear them talking around front. Out the window I saw more cars, more vans pulling up. It's a good thing I didn't drive over, would've never found a place to park. And Chloe still looked like hell.

'What?' I asked.

'Oh, it ain't… It's just no one ever called me sweetheart before. No one since.' And a wind blew through the open window, her hair all caught up in it. 'And I wanted to kiss him. When he said it. I wanted to kiss him.'

And, hell, what am I supposed to say to that?

When Ted came home that night and went straight to the kitchen for a beer, I knew better than to ask why. I'd been telling him for three months now, and I know his boss knows we're having a baby, so how hard could it be to request a little time off? He just can't bring himself to ask for it, though. Says it isn't customary. Damn custom to hell, I tell him, I ain't never done this parenting thing before and there's no way I'm going to start out doing it alone. He sat down on the couch and set the bottle on his knee.

'You see the news?' I pointed at the screen, though it was on the weather right then, but he knew what I meant. Ted and I have been together a while now.

'Yeah,' he said, and took a long drink. 'We skipped lunch to watch the coverage. Know Jed, the new kid?' Not really, but I said sure. 'Graduated with the daughter. You know, the… One of the victims.'

'Oh. Oh, Christ.' I put my hand on his wrist, but I don't think he noticed.

'Yeah. He, er. Had to go home. He couldn't be there, he couldn't watch. Couldn't work either, not with customers anyhow, and Chief's got all the new guys out on the lot, so…'

He tried to bring the bottle up for a drink and found my hand there, so I took it away, folded it with the other on my lap. The news cut to earlier footage of Chloe's neighbourhood, and I could just make out a sliver of her standing off to the right, in the flowers.

'You go over there?' he asked.

'I did. She was pretty shook up, acting funny. Forgetting herself, and saying the strangest things.' I smiled at him. 'Tell the truth I wasn't really sure what to say to her.'

He put down his beer and it was empty all of a sudden.

'What do you say to something like this.' He looked at my belly and put a hand there, though there wasn't much to feel yet. 'Something's wrong, when something like this can happen. Something dead wrong.'

I put my hand over his because, if there was a day to ask for a time off, I supposed it wasn't today. Poor Ted looked nearly as bothered as Chloe.

'You know, I should have asked her if she wanted to come here tonight, since we've got the pull-out couch in the office now.'

'You didn't offer?'

'I…' I stammered, he sounded so upset. 'It was chaos over there, all the news trucks and police. It slipped my mind, I guess.'

'Mary Jane!' he said, and got up fast to get the phone.

Once Chloe was settled in, she asked to see the nursery. She was still looking pretty shaky, and I didn't think she'd eaten anything yet, but I wasn't about to demur. I'd spent all week on that room, and anyhow it might do to cheer her up.

There wasn't an overhead light in the room and I hadn't found the right lamp yet, but some light came in from the street through the window, enough to see by. The window was open and the breeze was warm.

'Oh, wow,' she said.

'I know.'

Wasn't much to it yet, in the way of furniture anyhow. Just the one big dresser against the far wall. It'd been so much trouble to get it over from my sister's house, but worth it. It's old and dark, whorled wood. Imposing, sort of, with a heavy mood to it. Emily had it since we were teenagers and I'd thought, since Ted and I moved in here, that it would fit perfectly in this house. Only the dresser in the nursery so far, then, and the wallpaper I'd spent all week putting up. Chloe ran a hand over the wall.

'Oh, ain't that just darling. Are those poppies?'

'Tulips.'

'They're darling.'

She went to run a hand over the dresser. Gave me a smile when she recognized it.

'Thought I'd wait until after the shower to get anything else,' I said. 'Wishful thinking and all.'

'Probably a good idea.' Chloe was at the window. 'You know, I never noticed you could see my roof from up here. Away down the hill.' Her voice got quieter at every word. 'Can see the lights flashing down there.'

Unhealthy though it was for her to start talking like that again, I couldn't help standing next to her to look.

'They still got the police lights on? Neighbours can't appreciate something like that very much.'

'Just cameras flashing now,' she said, and pointed vaguely. 'And these big floodlights the news people set up. Whole block was lit up like Christmas when I left.'

I don't know why, but I took her hand. She rocked on her heels and came back to the room, looked around.

'Do you think,' she asked. 'Do you think those kids, their

parents ever even thought to be afraid of something like that, something so awful you don't even see it?'

Her hand dropped out of mine. I pulled shut the window and stepped back to give her a once-over. Chloe's big round eyes were always her best feature, but now they were squinted in an unbecoming way, like something had stung her. Her hair fell limp and straight, the colour of plywood. She looked back at me and seemed to find something distasteful, and then she just looked through me and at the baby, a look I wasn't used to yet, like I was just the incubator.

'Don't talk like that in here, Chlo,' I said. Away down the stairs Ted switched on the television and the noise drifted up to us. 'Have you eaten dinner?' I asked. She shook her head. 'There's plenty of jambalaya in the fridge. I can stick it in the stove for you.'

'I can get it,' she said.

'Well sprinkle some water over the top of it, from the tap will do, and preheat the oven. Around 350, shouldn't take too long. Oh, and it's in the little blue Tupperware bowl above the veggie crisper.'

'I'll find it,' she said, and left.

Down the stairs, over the television, I heard her talking to Ted. He answered lower, slower. They fell into a rhythm. The damn woman was never going to get anything nourishing in her before breakfast at this rate.

Next to the doorframe was the only part of the room I was unhappy with. The first day I started wallpapering I had no idea how to do it properly, and now there's a strip all full of air bubbles. A tulip bulged out into one of them and I stood in the doorway prodding it, careful not to break the surface with a fingernail. I could hear Ted and Chloe downstairs, and I heard the 11 O'clock Update intro music play on the television, but for the longest time I didn't step out of the nursery. For the life of me I couldn't make myself go downstairs to sit with them.

Lucky and Unlucky

L. E. Yates

All morning you've been lucky and unlucky. Yes, this is me. It's Lenny, your boyfriend. Lucky and unlucky. I've repeated these syllables so often that they have become the clack and the click of a train's wheels moving fast in a dark tunnel.

I can trace your morning with perfect transparency, perfect clarity of vision, until the point where you met me, and then I can tell it. On a mundane morning plucked out of a string of mundane mornings your alarm chirrups at 7 o'clock. You are sleeping on your side in the bed in your flat, heavily embroiled in a dream which sucks and nags at you and makes no sense; an old primary school teacher is there and a cat you have to take to a supermarket; you are in a canoe. The surreal aspects belie the fear and anxiety this is causing you. The alarm goes off and enters your dream. It takes you some seconds to struggle awake before you hit the off button and immediately lie down again. This is one of your favourite habits and has made you late for work countless times before. When I stay over this is my cue to chivvy you awake and out of bed, making a game of your sleepiness and my bullying. But I'm not there this morning as the night before I had to go to a work event and I went back to my own flat rather than crash in late and drunk.

Let's look at you for a moment – your dark hair is spread out in a loose wedge across the pillow. You look good. Your face has relaxed from the anxiety of the dream, and a crease from where you have slept too long on a wrinkle of the pillow only highlights how good your skin is and how young you are. You're only twenty-six, seven years younger than me. There is a thin slice of eye under your eyelids, which aren't quite closed, but not enough to reveal your dark irises, black like kalamata olives or those drops of pure, wet tar we saw outside your flat a month ago when the council resurfaced the street.

You've dragged yourself out of bed now. Unlucky. Outside on

159

the walkway you've just missed the postman's knock. He's wearing shorts because it is already a lovely morning (and because he is an optimist – you can tell from the way he whistles). He had two CDs and a couple of hardbacks from Amazon to offer you. But now he has put the cleverly constructed cardboard package back inside his bag as you pad naked into the bathroom. You piss, wipe yourself and throw the paper behind you. It misses the toilet and falls on the floor, a blossom of white paper, molded by your cunt and barely stained with urine. You skip a shower but roll deodorant on your armpits, gritting your teeth into a jagged animal expression as the deodorant catches one of the nicks from shaving your armpits last night.

As you are rolling on deodorant, a mile and a half away – down Mile End Lane, across the park, along St Philip's, past Mississippi Fried Chicken, the newsagent and the Church of the True Believers in God on Earth, two more small backstreets and then left – I have already got gingerly out of bed and kicked over a full glass of water I had considerately left there for myself last night. It soaked the library book sprawled face down with the spine cracked on the floor next to it. Unlucky. I wanted to take that with me to read on the journey into work but all I could do now is balance it on top of the radiator to dry. I don't have to be at work until ten but I had woken at six, my bladder swollen and rock solid, engorged with a froth of processed beer from last night. After I had opened my eyes and admitted consciousness on a trip to the toilet, I couldn't get back to sleep. Early morning light pushed through the thin protection of my blinds and outlined my clothes, the litter of books by the side of the bed and a wedge of door. My brain felt too big for my skull and I felt slightly sick so I had lain there quietly and let the minutes tick past me, using up the best part of the day, as my father would have said. When it got to seven, I couldn't bear the waiting, the remaining motionless like a frightened animal who hopes to ward off a hangover by hiding in stillness. I decided to leap out of bed and let it attack me with its full might.

I'm on the loo, not bothering to shave, when it occurs to me that I could meet you if I hurry. Sometimes our journeys into work converge and I've managed to catch you at the station a few times when you didn't know I was coming. Twice you looked thrilled and pecked kisses across my face in the middle of the station with the other commuters pushing past us. I grab a power bar and pour the cup of instant coffee I'd made myself down the sink. I snatch my suit jacket and leave the house.

Back in the bedroom you've shrugged on a shirt, and slipped into black trousers and your favourite pair of boots. You decide as you're dressing that you'll have to get breakfast on your way into work. From a place run by two Italians on the corner you can get a pastry and a latte. I know you like doing this because it makes you feel cosmopolitan, not the girl from Colchester any more. You're moving now with calm speed. Check your bag – diary, little bottle of water – shit, fill it up at the bathroom tap – tampons, foundation, little green purse, mascara, phone. You flick the fiddly clasp shut and you're out of the house, trying not to bang the door behind you. You know that other people are still asleep. You briefly wish you could be. You're nearly at the end of your street when you panic and think that you've forgotten your keys. This conjures up anger and frustration because you did this for the first time ever about two weeks ago and I had to leave work early and come across town, and because I'd had a row with some cunt in accounts that day I was sarcastic and patronizing when I arrived, your saviour. You fiddle with the clasp of your bag, stop in the street, and check the front compartments. The flash of metal reassures you that they are there. Lucky.

You look up, satisfied that your keys are safe, to see the red of the bus to the station flash past at the end of the street. There is no way you can sprint to the bus stop in time. Unlucky. You do the quick calculations of someone who travels the same route every morning and it confirms that you're going to be late.

You stand at the bus stop and wait. You want to buy a paper but don't want to risk missing another bus. The bus, as you think this, is one stop away but an old black woman with a shopping trolley is descending, slowly. You'll have enough time if you go now. You decide to go now and dart into the newsagent's just behind you. You grab a paper, hand over the right change and you're out of there just as the bus comes lumbering up the road to your stop.

I'm walking along the cool streets not yet beaten out with the day's sun. A few trees, blocked in by paving stones, rustle and their new growth shows up pale green. I'm swinging past the rows of yellowy-brown bricked houses. There's a man on the opposite side of the street, about a hundred and fifty metres ahead of me. He is looking for house numbers. He crosses over the street. Now I'm wrestling to remove my jacket because the walk is making me sweat and gnawing a corner of power bar, gripping it only with my teeth. I'm not thinking about either of these activities, I'm thinking about the top of my head. It looked okay in the mirror this morning but then it is hard to tell if you are losing your hair and even harder to see the top of your head properly in a mirror. I resolve to test the top of my head gently with my fingertips as soon as I've got a hand free.

I can see now (oh, the benefit of hindsight) that if I continue at this rate, I will collide with the black man in a tight collar and brown suit who is looking for an address. I mean collide, not just the casual brush past or clipping of shoulders that all Londoners are used to but a bone-shaking, head to head, sprawling in the gutter, full impact. I've just got to get my left sleeve off. The African guy looks down at a scrap of squared paper in his hand. There is a metre between us, one step for each of us, when he looks up and instinctively steps aside. The empty sleeve of my left jacket arm brushes against him and that is all. I don't even notice at the time. I'm walking jauntily off on my way to the station and somewhere behind me the African thinks he has found the right number on Belfield Avenue (although it eventually emerges that he wanted Belfield Road). Lucky – not to be sprawling on my bum in the middle of Belfield Avenue but to be cruising my way serenely onwards, having jettisoned the weight of ill fate, like the yacht that dumped Robert Maxwell overboard, until I'm within a few streets of the tube station.

Now you're on the bus. There aren't any seats but you don't care because it's only a short ride. You're clutching your bag with a newspaper under the same armpit you stung with deodorant earlier, and with the other arm you're clinging to the plastic light bulb dangling from the roof. You're not tall so this is an effort for you and rather than providing extra stability, it makes you stand on tiptoe, dangling almost suspended between the floor and the ceiling.

I can see the blue and red sign for the Underground across the street as I wait for the traffic lights to change. I just miss the green man. Across the road I see a bus pulling up but its rectangular frame blocks the stream of passengers from my view. I feel certain that you're on it as I fret for the flow of traffic to stop, for the lights to flick from one colour to another. A few people push past me and dart through the lanes of traffic, playing the gaps and nudges like a builder on a fruit machine, but I don't have the bottle today with my hangover so I wait on the curb.

You wait for people to filter off the bus, before stepping down onto the curb. You take twelve steps along the street and you disappear into the maw of the underground station.

When the lights change I push off the pavement, jostling along with the other commuters who had built up around me while I waited. Inside the tube station I swivel my head dramatically, searching for you, and the feeling that I'm a spy in a movie, charged with saving one girl amid a crowd, elevates me above my hangover. Unlucky. You're not by the downtrodden self-service machines, or at any of the ticket windows or at a cash machine. I can't see you talking earnestly to a guard or scanning the whiteboard for the current state of service. You don't appear to be at any of the barriers. You are already on your way to work, sucked into the tubes, or late, somewhere behind me.

I buy a ticket and head towards the barriers, all my haste and importance slowly deflating. People stream past me in the opposite direction. Now they are out in the air, surrounded by trees and light and sky while I'm waiting on the platform. The tug of stale air signals that a train is coming. I've just made it down the escalators and turned right onto the platform in time. Lucky.

You're ten metres away from me now. You've been waiting on the platform for longer than me, so you're leaning against the crimson red tile by the chocolate machine, your bag and newspaper drooping.

You look up for the train and instead you see me, partially hidden by a thicket of people. My suit and the fuzz of my blonde hair – it wasn't thinning as much as I'd worried – are enough to make you certain. People push forward and gamble on where the doors are going to stop.

'Lenny.' It's you and you distract me and I hold back. My face lights with pleasure.

'Catherine? Come on.' The carriage is heaving and when we try to shove on the people hardly yield.

'Shall we wait?' I ask

'I'm late already.'

I push on, bending my height and you fit into a gap between two people. The doors squeeze shut. There is someone's armpit in your face and a sharp object digging into my back. A rucksack? A shoulder bag? The train starts with a jerk and you would have fallen over were you not wedged between people. We grimace at each other and I blow you a kiss.

A flash. That's all it is. Like someone taking a photo indoors unexpectedly at a party but the irony is that it doesn't even hurt my eyes. I don't even have time to close my eyes against the light. It's funny. If I'd ever thought about this happening I would have pictured it in slow motion, giving me infinities and agonies of arched regret as my body tried to react away from the danger or heroically into it, shielding others. You can choose which version you prefer – for me it no longer matters. The world should slow down to allow me to cling to the last moments I'll ever have here. Precious for all their banality because that's all I'll ever have again and again and again and forever.

So, today you have been lucky and unlucky. A thousand tiny, infinite moments which add up to more than human beings can comprehend. A lattice of chance and causality laid bare, to be sifted in the weeks that follow. Lucky and unlucky, lucky and unlucky – these words are like a pulse in me that flickers on and off to the soft beep of your life support machine.

You've lost your right leg and a lot of your face. Your dark, soft skin that I so loved to touch was torn off. Your spleen and right kidney don't work any more. You won't be out of intensive care for nearly a year. You won't remember meeting me on the platform or even waking up that morning, so I've recorded it all carefully for you as best I could. You won't remember that kiss I blew you.

Road

Alistair Herbert

There was a straight, dusty road:
There was a family quarrel, there was a childless mother, there was a
setting sun. There were acres of cornfields and two girls in flowerprint
dresses laughing and splashing their ankles in a river I had been set to
cross but could not yet see. It was still ahead. Before these things on the
road there was a house, and inside the house a couple talking, while
outside a young boy threw a ball against the kitchen wall. And a little way
before the house stood a man clutching a battered black briefcase,
staggering along a dirt track to the only building on the horizon: Yes,
there was me.

It was the boy who saw me first, and escaped into the house in search of
his parents. Still at least thirty yards from the building, I heard no sound
from within before a door banged open and I lifted my head to see a tall
man, slight but handsome in shirt sleeves and jeans, approaching
cautiously. His dark hair was flecked grey. Behind him stood the boy,
made brave by the presence of his father and standing with hands on hips
as if it were he who owned the house. I opened my mouth to speak but
it was at that moment that my legs forsook me, and I sank to the ground,
still clutching the briefcase's worn handle as the world faded to black.

I woke on a sofa to the muted sounds of conversation in another room.
I tried to pull myself upright, but was stopped halfway by a young voice
coming from a chair in the corner.

'Father says you're not supposed to move 'til the doctor gets
here.'

I obeyed, dropping my head slowly back to the chair arm, and
turned on my side so as to look at the boy. He was sitting cross-legged
in a big, square armchair, head cocked to one side as he watched me.

'How long have you been watching me?'

He looked round at a clock on the wall. 'Two hours and forty-five minutes. Since you fell, outside. Father says you must be sick. Are you sick?'

'No, I don't think so. Just tired.'

'What happened?'

'There was an accident – a car accident – some way down the road. I walked from there.'

'Are you hurt? Who else was there?'

'No, I'm not hurt. Not badly.' I rotated my neck – it was aching. 'No, there was no one else there.'

'No other cars?'

'No, no other cars.'

'So how did you have an accident?'

I hesitated. 'I don't remember. I woke up and the car was in a ditch. I must have passed out.'

The boy seemed satisfied with this, and he fell silent for a short while. I took the opportunity to examine my surroundings – what little of them I could see. The house was old: old furniture, old wallpaper, greying pictures on the walls. The fireplace looked functional but unused, and there was no coal bucket. I tried to recall the man who must have carried me in, presumably the boy's father, but I was interrupted.

'What's your name?'

'Michael.'

'Michael What?' he giggled. I looked over at him.

'Michael Whitestone,' I replied, but he was too young to feel intimidated by my tone, and the inquisition continued almost without pause.

'Why were you coming to Clifton?'

'I wasn't coming here; I'm on my way somewhere else.'

'Where?'

'I'm going to meet someone.'

'Who?'

'An old friend of mine.'

'Why?'

'I like to visit my friends.'

He sat forward in his chair, leaning closer to me. His voice took on a hushed, conspiratorial tone. 'What's in your briefcase? Father...' Unable to stop myself I jerked upright and the boy retreated, watching my eyes as they skipped frantically across the room. '...Father says I shouldn't pry into other people's business, only I thought if you told me…' He fell silent and then offered, reproachfully, 'Father says you're not supposed to move,' before breaking off again. Regaining my composure, I sat down.

'I don't think I need a doctor. But I'd like to speak to your father – thank him for his help.'

The boy looked at me, hurt. 'I helped too.'

'Well thank you, too. You're very kind.' I rose and turned to the door, then back to face him. 'What's your name?'

'Jonah,' he replied with a smile. 'Jonah Matthews.'

'Well, Jonah, it was nice meeting you.' I left him shored up behind his crossed knees as I moved through the hall in search of the still-audible voices.

Quietly edging a door open, I saw my rescuer in a large, open kitchen, his hands planted on the dining table that occupied the central space. At the middle of the table lay my briefcase, shut but – I reasoned to myself – not necessarily unopened. There was a woman on the other side of the table, leaning back against the worktop with half-folded arms, her left hand drawn up to a creased forehead. Neither of them had noticed me When I entered, choosing the moment to announce my presence, both necks turned to show suspicious faces ever so briefly, before their owners regained control and adopted neutrality. The man moved back from the table, his body square to me, welcoming me into the room.

'So, you're awake,' he said. 'How are you feeling?'

In answer I reached up to my head, which was still spinning slightly, and forced a smile. 'Much better for a little rest, I think. I really can't thank you enough for your help.' Both man and woman made not-at-all gestures and noises at this, as I continued, 'if there had been no one here, or if you'd been even a little farther down the road, I don't know what I would have done.' A silence followed, before the woman interjected, almost in desperation,

'Would you like anything? A drink, or…' I quickly declined. She smiled, then looked to her husband nervously. He in turn looked at me, evidently just as unsure as his wife as to what came next. I decided to move things forward.

'Mr. Matthews, I presume,' I said, extending my right hand toward him. 'Michael Whitestone.' He took my hand, his firm grip somehow at odds with his obvious discomfort. 'I spoke to your son, I think,' I continued. 'Jonah.' He recovered quickly.

'Yes, that's right.' There was another pause. 'This is my wife, Helen.'

'Nice to meet you,' I smiled. She was a small woman, pretty in a plain way, quietly dressed and softly spoken. She smiled back at me, as Mr. Matthews motioned for me to take a seat, doing so himself at the far end of the table.

'I don't want to...' He paused and reconsidered the sentence. 'I'm sure you won't mind me asking what happened to you; what it was that led you to be on our road in such a state as you were.' He was speaking carefully; considering each word before he uttered it. He would make a useful contact, if not for the slightly rural accent: such voices weren't taken seriously. I watched his wife busying herself with something near the sink, though she was obviously listening intently for my response. I smiled again.

'To be honest I can't tell you much more than what you saw for yourself. One minute I was driving, the next I was coming round to find I had crashed. I was dazed, and my head was bleeding. I pulled myself from the car and started walking. Then I saw your house, or rather I heard the boy.' He nodded, taking in the information. 'I don't remember the crash itself,' I added, 'only waking up after it. I can't think how it happened.' Mr Matthews stayed silent before evidently reaching some sort of decision. His body relaxed noticeably, perhaps consciously.

'I'm sure Jonah told you I called a doctor,' – I began to protest but was waved silent – 'and I want you to see him. I don't want to worry that we didn't look after you well enough. In the meantime Helen is cooking... Don't try and be polite, there's no shortage. You're our guest, and we must treat you well.' I wondered at this joviality, so soon after such obvious unease, as I thanked him. I asked if I might use the bathroom, and as he stood to lead me to the stairs I reached out and picked up my briefcase from the table. Two pairs of eyes followed my hand's movement, and I looked up in time to see genuine panic in Helen's eyes. It was there for less than a second before the bland expression returned, but it told me what I needed to know. The briefcase had been opened.

After using the toilet I turned on the taps and went about opening the briefcase and removing its contents. Everything was still there. One by one I removed sheets of paper, crumpled them and crunched it all into the basin. I took a book of matches from my breast pocket, lit one and held it to the nearest bundle. Flames rose between curling rolls and licked towards the centre of the bowl. As the fire gained strength, spears of blue and green started to whisper up among the orange and the whole was reflected in a mirror above the basin, violent and alive, in which I saw for a moment my own face. I looked old all of a sudden. Old and tired. I wondered how long I had been ageing without allowing myself to see it; the face in this mirror did not seem to correlate with the face I thought of as my own. Pulling my mind back, I looked around the room until my eyes fell on a square wicker laundry basket, which I dragged to the centre of the tiled floor as the fire continued to burn, blackening the wall behind it and obscuring the ceiling with dark, choking smoke.

Standing on the basket's solid lid with cord from the blinds connecting my neck to the light fitting, I watched as the fire began to ebb. It had not possessed the power to consume the house, but it had served its purpose. In the hallway I could hear footsteps and commotion; a police siren wailed outside the frosted window, and lights flashed. There was banging on the door, and a woman's voice shouting. I had been right, then. I had made the right decision.

The sky was darkening rapidly now, and a chill draft was creeping in through that window. It felt soft against my fingers, fighting with the heat from the basin. I realised I had not discovered Mr Matthews' first name, and decided to christen him Benedict. Benedict Arnold, perhaps. The door would break soon, I knew. I looked across at the mirror again but could no longer see my face. The door would break soon. The last flames were dying: the papers were shrivelled, their stories lost. The door would break soon. There was one story remaining. I closed my eyes and I was a mountain top. Touching the wind, kissing the clouds, I saw a familiar ghost. He smiled at me, and he pushed my body forward, and I acquiesced, and I fell. But now I'm lying again: there was no mountain, and there was no push. I kicked out, and I fell. I fell into the breeze.

Contributors

Anna Ball is writing a PhD thesis in cultural theory at the University of Manchester, where she also works as a teaching assistant in the English department. She is the editor of *ManuScript*, an academic journal in Literary Studies. She has another story in the forthcoming Redbeck Press anthology.

Suzanne Batty is a poet and co-editor the Manchester magazine *Rain Dog*. The Poetry Business published her pamphlet *Shrink* in 1997, and she is working on her first collection 'The Barking Thing'.

Paul Brownsey was once a newspaper reporter in Luton, Bedfordshire, and is now a lecturer in philosophy at Glasgow University. He finds the mindset required for writing fiction entirely different from that required for academic writing. He lives in Bearsden, on the outskirts of Glasgow.

John Carnahan is a student at the University of Wales, Aberystwyth, and a lecturer at California State University, East Bay. His fiction and criticism has appeared in *The Comics Journal, The Misfit Library,* and *On the Page.* He can't carry a tune in a bucket.

Graham English is currently studying creative writing at Kent University.

Tracey Emerson has lived in Edinburgh for ten years, working as a performer and workshop leader in theatre and community arts. She started writing prose fiction in 2003 and in 2004 was a runner up in *The Scotsman* and Orange Short Story Award.

Crysta Ermiya is of Filipino and Turkish-Cypriot parentage, originally from London and now living in Newcastle-upon-Tyne. She is a co-editor of *Other Poetry* magazine and runs indie poetry press Dogeater. Her stories have been published on Pulp.net (2006) and in *Wonderwall* (Route, 2005).

Thomas Fletcher was born in Worcester in 1984 and grew up in Cumbria. In 2005 he achieved a First Class BA in Creative Writing from the University of Leeds, and has since divided his time between Leeds and Cumbria whilst working on a novel and a collection of short stories.

Alistair Herbert grew up in Leek and graduated from the University of Manchester in 2005. He currently works in Stretford and is writing for several projects, among them a novel and a collection of pop songs. He is 21 years old.

Paul Hocker's neighbours, Emily and Sarah, said: 'He once told us he used to be an actor and was in *The Bill* for 12 episodes but we checked on the internet and he was lying. Paul is noisy at night and has participated in four vast Catholic romances.'

Alice Kuipers was born in London and now lives in Saskatoon, Canada, where she works as a Pilates teacher. She has had stories published in literary magazines and produced for CBC radio. She is a graduate of MMU.

Adam Marek was born in 1974, and has been writing fiction since his teens. After leaving film school he worked in the music video industry, but is now part of the editorial team at the Royal Society for the Protection of Birds. His stories have been runners up and second prize winners in the Bridport Prize. He lives in Bedfordshire with his wife and sons.

Melanie Mauthner's first piece of fiction 'Prudence' was published in *My Cheating Heart* (Honno, 2005). Her short story 'The Lido' won first prize in Lambeth's 'Impressions of Brixton' competition in 2003. She also writes non-fiction and her most recent book is *Sistering* (Palgrave, 2005). She lives in South London.

Andy Murray has worked as a film reviewer, collaborated on several short films, and written a biography of TV scriptwriter Nigel Kneale (Headpress). His story 'One Down' appeared in Comma's *Manchester Stories* 7. He is currently working on an academic study of TV writer Russell T Davies.

Gabriella Reed is Filipino-American and was born in Madison, Wisconsin in 1985. She is currently a short-term student of English at the University of Kent in Canterbury.

C.D. Rose is from Manchester but currently lives in the south of Italy, where he enjoys not feeling at home. He spends far too much time writing improbable short stories about fish, shoes, ships, jewels, paintings, photographs, violins, cats, kites, big cities, small towns, bets, promises, deals, dreams, thefts, displacement, exile, love, loss and death.

Mandy Sutter, who can see Ilkley moor from every window of her house, is currently Writer-in-Residence for Leeds Teaching Hospitals Trust. Her poems and short stories have appeared in literary magazines and on BBC

Radio 4. Recent publications include two stories in *Are You She?* a women's showcase anthology published by Tindal Street Press last year.

Pat Winslow worked for twelve years as an actor before leaving the theatre in 1987 to take up writing. Her poetry collections include *Skin & Dust* (Blinking Eye), *The Girl in the Iron Lung* (Crocus), the *Fact of an Eye* (Amazing Colossal) and *Harvest* (Jackson's Arm).

Ann Winter teaches English Language and Literacy to adult and teenage asylum seekers in West London. She has been writing fiction since completing a research MA in experimental fiction in 2003.

L.E. Yates grew up in Manchester and has a degree from Cambridge University in English Literature. She is currently taking an MA in Creative Writing at UEA, and finishing her first novel, based on the life of an eighteenth century Scottish poet and forger, James Macpherson.

Acknowledgements

Although only one person is officially ISBN-ed as the editor of this anthology, equal thirds of the credit should go to Comma's co-founder Sarah Eyre and Jim Hinks for their tireless work during a mammoth selection process. Special thanks should also go to Tim Cooke and assistant editor Maria Crossan, for their continued contribution throughout the year. Much of the introduction responds to articles and essays collected in two books – *Short Story Theories* (Ohio, 1977) and *New Short Story Theories* (Ohio, 1994), both edited by Charles E. May – to which the editor is indebted. Comma would also like to thank Will Carr and Dale Hicks for their faith and enthusiasm, as well as Maria Roberts for her keen eye, Ike Shaffer for a certain visit to Leeds railway station, and Zoe Lambert for her elicit trade in university library books (they're on their way back).

]